Love Is
Blind

Kyoshi

DEDICATION

This book is dedicated to all the ladies out there that are going through domestic violence or have been through it. Get out before it's too late, tell someone, don't be ashamed. You have a voice, let it be heard. *What you think is love, is truly not, need to elevate and find...Love Is Blind...*
Keep your head up mamas!

ACKNOWLEDGMENTS

First and foremost I thank **God** for this gift, without Him nothing is possible. He gave me a gift I never knew I had. I'm forever grateful for His continuous blessings in my life.

My pride and joy, my heartbeat, my everything, my reason for living **Ky'Shawn Syncere**, everything I do is for you. You are my motivation when times get tough and I wanna quit. I truly thank God for you, I love you more than life itself.

My baby girl **Kyana La'Shae**, no you're not mine biologically, but I've been honored to be a part of your life for the last seven years. I love you as if I birthed you myself.

My grandparents **Barbara and Johnny**, I love you guys to life! Thank you for your wisdom and your love! For keeping me on the right path and giving me stern love and guidance.

My mother **Adrienne**, thank you for all your life lessons and teaching me to be a strong independent black woman. No matter what you went through, you always kept us in line. You taught me to never give up. I love you very much.

My big sister **Kimbria**, we fuss and fight but I wouldn't trade you for anybody in this world. Love you to pieces!

My second set of parents **Daphne and Eric Faison**, words can't express how much I love and appreciate you guys! You may have lost a son, but you gained a daughter and a bad little boy (lol).

My Baby Daddy (lol) **Da'Shawn**, we been rocking together for alot of years, seven to be exact. Through the ups and downs you've been by my side. You've be there for me since day one and gave me the greatest gift ever, our kids. I don't know what the future holds for us, but I love you! Never change kid, your parents raised a great man.

My best friend/sister **Jettina**, words can't express how much you mean to me. You have been there for me through it ALL! Thank you for your encouragement and continued support. I love you more than you'll ever know.

My big brothers **Eric & Derrell**, I love you guys sooooooo much! Thank you for never changing and always being there no matter how much time passed. I'm so proud of the men you have become, keep leading by example.

To my guardian angel, my best friend, my big brother **Antonio E.**

i

Williams. Not a second of any day goes by that you don't cross my mind, I miss you more than anyone will ever know. Until we meet again, continue to watch over me. I carry you in my heart everyday and I love you very much. Continue to rest in peace my love.

My girl **Jenea**, thank you for being a listening ear whenever I needed to vent, even though I'm the better employee, lol (insider)! I am grateful for our friendship, love ya chick!

My girl **Janelle** thank you for all the laughs! I am so grateful that you were placed in my life, you truly have become a great friend. I got alot of love for you chica!

My Biomerieux fam **David (the president, lol), Anthony Wells (big hands!), Alex (my buddy), Jamar (talkin tom, lol), Ms Emma (tell it like it is), Ms Maggie (VERY outspoken), Diane (crazy ass, lol), Cici (bridges, lol), Brenda (off the damn chain, lol), Warren (still my boo, lol), Carlton (strong man), Twizz (You should've been a comedian! Keep that music poppin!)** I miss yall sooooooooo much! You meet people in life that make a lasting impression on you and you all did that for me. I got a lot of love for you and I'll forever cherish the good days and those to come! David, I promise not to use any of your "material" in my books (Lol)!

My cousin **Nikia** thank you for always being there for me! I love me some you!!!!!

My cousins **Eboni & Brittani**, thanks for never changing and always being you! We're more than cousins, we're "Johnny's Pride" (Lol) I love you pudding pops!

My bestie **Will**, thanks for always being you! We connected on a level that I never thought we would, I'm proud to call you my bestie! I got nothing but love for you big head! Thank you and your wife for the support!

Leondra Williams, my publisher/friend words can't express how grateful I am for you! You believed in me from the very beginning, I never saw myself as an author but you took a chance on me and for that I will forever be grateful! Thank you for being patient with me and pushing me, I am thankful for all that you do! I am proud to call you not only my publisher, but also my friend! I'm rocking with you forever and a day, Love ya girl!

Alicia Hartley, my publisher thank you so much for the opportunity to be a part of DDP, I am forever grateful!

David Weaver thank you for accepting me with open arms and giving me this opportunity. I respect the man you are and all that you do! You have a big heart, with big dreams and I'm glad to be apart of the squad. I got nothing but love for you sir! I heard it was Cheque Running season?

My "Cousin" **Denora** , words can't express my gratitude for you! Thank your for your continous support and encouragement! The laughs sometimes keeps me going and I appreciate it! Love you lady!

My girl **Ciara,** still can't believe you're gone, but I'm glad you don't have anymore pain. You rocked with me even before you joined the squad and I got nothing but love for you boo... Watch over us from up there in Heaven and I'll see you when we meet again... RIP Lady!

My homie **Azor aka "Ace",** still so hard to believe that you're gone. I miss you so much! All the laughs and memories we shared, I'll carry in my heart forever. I love you big baby! RIP Polly Grandson!

My **DDP & TBRS family**, thank you for accepting me into the family. I truly appreciate you all, I got nothing but love for ya'll! #TBRS4LYFE

This story came to me out of nowhere, but I'm glad it did. Domestic violence is very real and I feel as though it isn't talked about enough. I haven't personally experienced it, but I know those who have. My hope is for anybody that reads this book and is going through domestic violence, I pray that this book touches you. Get out before it's too late!

Without further a do, I present to you; Love is Blind...

To those I didn't mention, charge it to my head and not my heart. I love you all!.

PROLOGUE

What's up y'all? My name is Kaylen Monaé Gibson-Lassiter. I'm a 26-year-old wife to an amazing man, a mother to a precious baby girl named Kadence and a baby boy named RJ. I decided to let y'all into my world for a minute because I got so tired of seeing my young sistas going through the same things that I went through with a man. Men, this is for y'all too because a lot of you THINK you know how to love a woman, but you really don't. It took me a while to learn how a man is supposed to truly love a woman; in fact it took me almost ten years to escape hell on earth. I used to be ashamed of the things I went through and then I realized that my story could help somebody else, so I decided to turn my test into a testimony. So sit back and enter my world and let me tell you my story.

CHAPTER ONE

The Beginning

"Come here bitch," I heard my father say to my mother as she screamed.

"I'm sorry Steve, I'll fix it." My mother, Karen, cried.

"Don't try to fix it now, I see I'm gone have to teach you a lesson," he said evilly.

At thirteen years old, this was something that I was used to in my household. My mother stayed at home and took care of the house while my father worked downtown as a sheriff. If his food wasn't cooked to his liking then he beat her, if his uniform wasn't pressed like he liked it, she got beat. Hell, if the wind blew the wrong way he would beat my mother.

I always wondered why she stayed. One minute he would be beating her ass and then two hours later they would makeup and were cuddled up on the couch. So in my young mind, I thought that was love, I mean, why else would she stay?

I would go in my room and silently cry because I got so tired of hearing my mother beg and plead for him to stop. So as another fight went down in the Gibson household, I put my headphones in and began to write in my journal.

I grew up in Raleigh, North Carolina. I didn't have any siblings or any friends. I'm what you would call a loner. I'm quiet, and I like to stay to myself. I often found myself wanting to tell somebody what was going on, but then I would remember my mother's words, "What goes on in this house, stays in this house," and I would just keep my mouth shut.

I always felt like everyone knew what was going on in our house. I guess that's why I stayed to myself because I didn't want anybody judging my mother. Daddy did keep a roof over our head, made sure we had nice things and he never laid a finger on me. In fact, he treated me the exact opposite of how he treated my mother.

I was his princess, the apple of his eye and definitely his twin. My father was a handsome man, at thirty-five, he stood at six feet, 235 pounds, and had smooth dark chocolate skin with brown almond shaped eyes, close cut with deep waves and a gorgeous smile.

My mother, on the other hand, was five foot six, 170 pounds, light skin, hazel eyes, short cut hair, and a thick frame with wide hips. She was absolutely breathtaking and what most would consider a redbone. It always amazed me that they could fight all night long. You would never know it if you weren't there.

See, with daddy being a cop, he knew where to hit her and where not to hit her.

"Kaylen come here," I heard my daddy call out to me an hour after their daily fight.

"Yes daddy?" I said softly as I entered to living room with my head down.

"Go ahead in the kitchen and eat baby."

As I entered the kitchen, I found my mother fixing our plates in silence with her head down. The moment she lifted her head, I knew that something was wrong because her eye was swollen and started to turn black. Daddy had never hit her in the face before, so why would he start now? I asked myself.

"Karen, you got thirty seconds to bring me my got damn plate!"

My father's booming voice caused both of us to jump as she hurried out of the kitchen with his food.

CRASH!

"Bitch, didn't I tell you to cut up my steak," he yelled and threw the plate up against the wall.

"I'm sorry, Steve, I'll fix you another one," she cried.

"Don't bother, I swear you ain't good for nothing," he said before he grabbed his jacket and keys, and slammed the door on his way out.

I got up from the table and entered the living room to find my mother on her hands and knees as she picked up the broken plate and food. I went and grabbed the trashcan and got down to help her. She stopped and looked at me momentarily, then grabbed me and held me tight.

"I'm so sorry, baby," she said over and over again.

That night, I lay with my mother, and we fell asleep together. I didn't fully understand what was going on, but I hated how my father hurt my mother. But what could I do? I was only a kid, and obviously this was love. Otherwise she would've left, right?

CHAPTER TWO

After that night, things went from bad to worse. I mean, it got to the point when daddy wouldn't even come home, and sometimes he brought his mistress to the house. Yep, you read it correctly, his mistress. Mommy wouldn't even say anything. She would just take it, so it got to the point where I stopped caring. If she didn't care why should I? That's what love is, right?

I was starting to become a woman, and I finally started to come out of my shell. I had met Kapri Thompson my freshman year of high school, and we had become close over the last two years. She was a year older than me and had become the big sister I always wanted.

Kapri was ok as far as looks went; she stood at five foot seven around 150 pounds, light skin with big brown eyes and short hair. She had an ok body but nothing to write home about.

By the time I turned sixteen, I had filled out like a grown woman, and men were starting to take notice. I stood at five foot three, 145 pounds, brown skin, hazel eyes and dark brown hair that stopped just below my shoulder blades with hips and ass for days.

It was my junior year just before Christmas when I met Black. It was a day I would never forget. Kapri and I decided to go to the homecoming game. I had never been to a football game before, so I was excited.

The game was held on a Friday night, so I got permission to stay over Kapri's house for the weekend. We decided to dress alike, something we often did. I decided to wear a pink fitted tee shirt with a pair of acid washed Levis, pink flight jacket with my pink and white reebok classics. Pri had on the same outfit, but hers was purple.

When we pulled up to the school it was PACKED! There were nice whips lined up everywhere, and everybody was just chilling not really paying attention to the game.

As we were walking toward the gate to purchase our tickets, I heard somebody call out to Pri.

"Who dat?" she asked as she searched the sea of faces.

"This Black, girl," he replied as he approached us.

"Oh shit, what's good baby," she said hugging him.

"Ain't shit, I saw you, and I had to come speak."

"Yea I bet," she smirked as she peeped the way he is eyeing me. "Where ya boy at," she asked.

"He over there with the crew, how 'bout you and your friend come chill with us for a minute?" He suggested as he smiled at me and caused me to blush.

"You got some cannabis?" She asked.

"And you know it," he smirked.

"You down with that, Kay," she asked as she looked at me, and I just shrugged letting her know that it was up to her.

As we made our way toward the rowdy bunch, Black took that moment to introduce his self.

"What's good with you lil mama, I'm Black," he introduced himself holding out his hand.

"Kaylen," I responded softly shaking his hand.

"Oh shit, look who done stepped in the muthafuckin place," some guy with a mouth full of gold yelled as we approached.

"Boogie, sit yo overly hyped up ass down," Black shouted causing everybody to laugh.

"Who your friend, Pri?" Another guy asked eyeing me.

"This is Kaylen, Kaylen meet my niggas Tre, Twon, Nice, Rico and Boogie," Black responded before she could, and I waved at them.

I sat quietly watching them drink and pass a blunt around, I looked to my left and saw Kapri sitting on Rico's lap.

"You always this quiet," Black asked me leaning up against his old school box Chevy.

"Yea, when I'm around people I don't know." I told him softly.

"Well, what's it gonna take for you to feel comfortable around me?"

I shrugged.

"Well, how about this, my name is Cordae, but everybody calls me Black. I'm twenty-three, single and I don't have any kids," he said.

"Ok, well, I'm Kaylen, I'm sixteen, I'll be seventeen on Christmas Day, and I'm in my junior year at Clayton High," I replied shyly.

"It's nice to meet you, Kaylen," he said smiling.

Black was quite handsome. He stood at six foot three, 215 pounds, dark as night with almond shaped brown eyes, and the prettiest set of teeth I had ever saw on a man.

For the rest of the night, I became acquainted with Black. But if I knew then, what I know now, I would've saved myself a lot of heartache.

CHAPTER THREE

After that night at the homecoming game, Black and I became inseparable. I know you're thinking, "What does a twenty three year old man want with a sixteen-year-old girl?" The answer was simple. See, Black knew that I was sheltered, and he wanted to control me.

I ain't gone lie though, it started out amazing. Black showed me things I'd never seen before, and with things being so bad at home and only getting worse, he was my escape. The first two years we were together, Black and his crew came up. They were trafficking all over North Carolina and even out of state. Anything I wanted, Black got me before I could even ask for it, and in return I gave him my virginity along with my heart.

He even took me to my senior prom. When my mother met him, she instantly didn't like him, but he and daddy got along great.

We dated for those two years before shit got bad. It seemed

that the more money Black made, the worse he became. After I graduated and turned eighteen, I left home and moved in with Black even though my mother begged me not to. I was young and in love. There wasn't shit you could tell me about Black. If I knew then, what I know now, I would've taken heed to my mother's words.

I remember the day I left home very clearly...

"Kaylen, please don't move in with that boy," my mother pleaded, but her pleas fell upon deaf ears as I continued to pack.

"He loves me, and I love him, whether you like it or not I'm leaving," I told her as I continued to throw my things into my suitcases.

"Something ain't right about that boy. He ain't no good for you. Kay. That boy gone hurt you bad baby," she warned.

"Oh, you mean like daddy ain't no good for you, and he hurts you? Black doesn't treat me bad mama, he loves me, and I'm leaving," I smartly responded before I could catch myself. *"I'm sorry,"* I said softly after I saw the hurt expression across her face.

"I'm gone say this and then I'll be on my way, because I can tell your mind is made up. Your father and I have horrible issues, I can admit that. It didn't start out like that though, baby, your father swept me off my feet, and I loved him more than I loved myself. It didn't get bad until your father's partner, Jon, was killed in the line of duty. He blamed himself for it and took his frustrations out on me. I probably should have left a long

time ago, but I stayed for you, as crazy as that may sound. I grew up without a father, and I didn't want that for you.

My mother told me the same thing about your father that I'm telling you about that boy, and I didn't listen. I was young and in love, I was determined to prove her wrong. The very first time he hit me I heard my mother's words clear, but what could I do? Going back and having her say 'I told you so' was not an option, so I stayed and endured it. I even distanced myself from my family. I kept thinking, it's gonna get better. I just gotta learn how to keep him happy and not make him so angry. All these years I blamed myself for him hitting me, so I kept quiet about it. He provided for us and gave us stability, so I equated that with love. Kaylen, I lost my self-respect and dignity. It took me fifteen years to get tired and finally see what everybody else saw a long time ago.

So, I'm leaving your father today. I want you to have my car. That way you'll be able to get around without depending on anybody. It ain't much, but it's paid for. I'm going back down to Augusta with my sister, and you're welcome to join me if you want. As your mother, I love you with everything in me, and I'll always be here for you. Just don't become anybody's fool, ok? Most importantly, never ever lose you in a man," she told me with tears rolling down her face as she hugged me tightly and left the bedroom.

I sat down on my bed with tears in my eyes and thought on everything my mother had said. A part of me wanted to go with *her, in fact I heard a small voice that said "go", but the biggest part of me wanted to stay with my man.*

"Lord give me a sign," I prayed quietly.

My phone rang...

"Hello."

"Hey baby, you ready for me to come get you," Black asked me.

"Yea, I'm just finishing up," I replied, and instantly the conversation I had with my mother was forgotten.

I asked for a sign, and I got it. I was going to be with my man. I grabbed my things and headed toward the front door where I saw a taxi waiting.

"Ok baby, I'm gone. You remember what I said, you hear? Any time you want to come, you don't even have to call, just come on. I'll call you when I land. I love you, Kaylen," she said as she embraced me

"I love you too, ma," I told her, and just like that she was gone.

Not long after mommy left, Black arrived in his red old school box Chevy on 24s. After loading my things into the car, I hopped in mommy's car, and we were off to start our new life together.

Black's house was located in the county of Garner, it had three bedrooms, two full baths, a spacious kitchen, two car garage, and a huge backyard with an in ground pool. It was so quiet out here, and the nearest neighbor was about a half mile down.

"I love it out here, baby," I told Black as we sat on the patio smoking a blunt, another habit I picked up.

"Me too ma, it's quiet and peaceful."

That night Black made love to me all over the house. He brought me to ecstasy over and over again. I was sprung, and it wasn't shit anybody could tell me about my man, he had me gone. Life was great, but nothing could've prepared me for the hell I would soon endure.

CHAPTER FOUR

I ended up getting an academic scholarship to North Carolina Central University in Durham, North Carolina where I decided to study Psychology with a concentration in neuroscience. The first day of school was hectic. The campus was huge, and I had a hard time getting from class to class.

"You need some help?" I heard a smooth voice ask from behind me as I searched for my General Psychology class.

"Yes please, I'm trying to find Professor Brinson's class," I replied.

I turned around to find a six-foot Greek God!

"Ok, well his class is in the Psychology building. I was actually headed that way. I could walk you," he offered, and I agreed.

"Julian Green," he said holding out his hand.

"Kaylen Gibson," I replied as I accepted his hand into mine.

"Nice to meet you, Kaylen."

When I tell you this man was fine, I mean fine with a capital F! Homeboy was six five, about two hundred and thirty pounds, caramel skin, light green eyes, his tapered hair is curly and looked so soft, and he had the brightest smile I'd ever seen.

"I take it this is your first year?" He asked as we walked across campus.

"What gave me away?"

"The fact that you were looking for a Psychology class in the Biology building," he replied and caused me to laugh.

"I'm guessing you're an upper classman," I asked.

"Yea, I'm in my third year, and I'm a Law major," he replied as we entered the Psychology Building.

"Well, here we are."

He stopped in front of what I assumed was Professor Brinson's class.

"Thank you so much for your help, it would've taken me all day to find it," I told him as I smiled at him.

"No problem, glad I could help."

He looked at me, and I blushed.

"I guess I'll see you around," I told him as I grabbed the doorknob to enter the class, but he lightly grabbed my arm.

"If you're not busy after your classes, I know a nice little coffee shop around the corner, maybe you would like to join me?"

"I wish I could, but I have to get home right after," I told him, and I instantly saw the disappointment flash across his face.

"Ok, well, I guess I'll see you later."

I nodded as I made my way into the classroom finding a seat near the back. I could barely focus on anything the professor was saying because Julian kept crossing my mind. This is the first time I'd ever thought about any other man besides Black, and as crazy as it sounded, that frightened me a little.

I shook Julian from my mind and focused on the lecture. My class load ended around four, and I was exhausted. All I wanted to do was go home and take a long nap. The commute from school to home was hectic. I got caught in the rush hour traffic on I-40, and I didn't get home until 5:45.

"Where the fuck you been," Black barked as soon as I stepped foot into the house.

"I've been at school, but you knew that already, and why are you yelling?" I asked him sitting my books down on the coffee table.

"Your classes ended at 4:00, it's damn near six, and you just getting here. Now where the fuck you been?" He continued to yell.

"My classes did end at four, but the traffic on 40 was hectic. Why are you tripping?" I asked as I rolled my eyes and walked into the kitchen.

This was a side of Black that I had never seen before, but it was one that I would become all too familiar with in the coming years.

"Don't fucking walk away from me when I'm talking to you,"

Black snapped as he entered the kitchen where I had started dinner.

"You want to argue, or you want to eat?" I asked him smartly.

In a flash Black was up on me with his hand around my neck.

"Don't fucking get smart with me, Kay. Let it take your ass two hours to get home again, and I'm gone fuck you up," he gritted, squeezing my throat as I looked at him with wide eyes and began clawing at his hands. "You hear me," he shouted angrily.

I could only nod as my eyes start to water. He finally let me go, and I fell to the floor gasping for air.

"Now, get the fuck up and fix me something to eat. By the time I get back, my shit better be on the table," he demanded as he grabbed his keys off the counter and slammed the door on his way out.

I was laying on the floor momentarily stunned. That was my first sign to exit, but I didn't take heed. Instead I got up off the floor and started cooking dinner.

CHAPTER FIVE

I didn't see Black for two days after that incident, and when he finally decided to come home, he came in with a new outfit on smelling like Ivory soap. I didn't say anything or question him about where he had been. He bought me a diamond tennis bracelet and apologized, he told me that he was stressed. He promised that it would never happen again, and of course, I accepted his apology, and we had a mind blowing makeup sex session.

For the rest of the week, I made sure to leave school at exactly 4:00. I avoided Julian like the plague; whenever I saw him I would go the other way. I even learned a back way that would get me home faster bypassing the highway. All was well in our home until about two weeks later.

One Saturday while Black was out, I decided to catch up on the laundry and some other housework. I was separating the clothes when I came across a t-shirt of his with red lipstick on the bottom of it, so I placed it to the side. I checked the pockets of the jeans I found, and in them was a piece of paper with a number and 'Laila' written on it with a red lipstick kiss on the bottom. It was the same shade that was on his shirt, and my blood started to boil. I contemplated on what I should do. I decided to call Kapri and get her advice.

"Hey girl," she said as soon as she answered.

"Hey Pri, what you doing?" I asked her.

"Not shit, about to go do some shopping."

"I need some advice. I found a number in Black's jeans, what should I do?" I asked her biting my bottom lip, something I did when I was pissed.

"You trippin' because you found a number? Girl, he's a man, they cheat. My advice to you is to throw it away and don't say shit about it," she responded.

I looked at the phone in disbelief.

"Are you serious right now?" I asked her.

"Look Kay, you got a good nigga that provides for you and gives you whatever you want, as long as he don't bring that shit to your door, let it go. He's a hustler, and that shit comes with the territory. Stop acting like a little girl. You go looking for shit, you end up finding it, and you might not like what you find. I gotta go," she said and hung up before I could say anything else.

She on some other shit. I'll be damned if I sit by and knowingly let my man cheat on me. So I decided to call Miss

Laila and see what she had to say. I dialed the number, and my hands were literally shaking.

"Hello."

"Yes, can I speak to Laila," I asked.

"This is she, who's this," she replied.

"You don't know me, but my name is Kaylen, and I'm Black's girlfriend. I was calling because I want to know why I found your number in his pants pocket."

"Well, it seems to me that you need to be calling your so called man, sweetie, not me," she smugly replied.

"He's not here, so I'm asking you, woman to woman." I said as I began to lose my cool.

Before she could respond I heard an all too familiar voice

"Hang up the phone, baby. I need to feel you on daddy dick."

"Well, I gotta go, my man's calling," she said before hanging up in my ear.

I feel my chest tighten, and I start to hyperventilate.

"Why would he do this to me?" I asked myself trying to regulate my breathing.

Tears streamed down my face, and I fell to the floor. After picking myself up off the floor, I continued to wash the clothes almost in a daze. After I finished, I lay across the bed and cried myself to sleep.

"Kaylen!" I heard Black scream my name from downstairs, but I didn't respond as I got up and went into the bathroom.

"Kaylen, you don't hear me talking to you," he asked as he

entered the bathroom.

I still hadn't said a word. I turned to walk out of the bathroom when I felt him grab my hair and pulled me back.

"The fuck is your problem? You don't hear me talking to you?" he yelled as he tightened his grip on my hair.

In one movement he pulled me down to the ground literally dragging me out of the bathroom.

"Stop Black," I screamed as I felt the carpet burning my skin as he dragged me through the room.

"Oh, so you can talk now?" He asked sarcastically before he threw me into the wall so hard, pain hit me instantly. "And you going through my shit now? I see I gotta teach you not to fuck with shit that don't belong to you," he said as he came toward me as I attempted to crawl away.

He grabbed my hair, hit me hard in my side, then again in my back; over and over again with his fists.

"I'm sorry," I cried weakly, curled up in a fetal position on the floor.

"Nah, I don't think you sorry yet, but you will be," he responded, as he grabbed my throat and squeezed tight as I clawed at his hands.

"Now, I'm only gonna tell you this once. Stay out my shit and stay in your fucking place, you understand?" he asked through clenched teeth.

He released me just as I felt myself about to pass out.

"I said do you understand?"

I could only nod.

"Good, now clean yourself up and go make me some food."

As he left out, I sat on the floor in pain. I got up slowly and headed to the bathroom. I looked into the mirror. I saw handprints embedded in my neck, lifted my shirt and saw bruises all over my torso and back.

I silently cried and asked God, "Why is this my life?"

I slowly made my way into the kitchen and cooked something to eat. After I finished cooking, I made us both a plate.

"Who is this other plate for," he asked me as he sat at the table.

"Me," I softly replied.

"Nah, you don't get to eat tonight. Matter of fact, go to bed," he said harshly, after he took the plate and dumped the whole thing in the garbage.

I silently made my way upstairs and ran me a hot bath. My side and back hurt so bad that I knew I had a few injured ribs. Taking my clothes off was a task within itself. It took me a full ten minutes to completely remove my clothes.

As I eased my way into the tub, I heard my mother's words clearly, and all I could do is weep. *If I leave, where would I go? Down south with mom? Or back home with daddy? Nah, I'm not up for the "I told you so" speech. I'm gonna stay here and work on these issues with my man. I just gotta stop making him so angry,* I said to myself. Yea, that's it; from this day forward, I'll be the best woman to him that I can be.

CHAPTER SIX

As I slowly made my way to class, I heard my name being called.

"Kaylen, wait up," Julian yelled, and I had stopped to let him catch up.

"Hi Julian," I greeted.

"You are one hard woman to track down," he said smiling at me as we began to walk.

"I'm not that hard to find, maybe you just weren't looking hard enough."

"You got jokes I see."

He lightly bumped my shoulder causing me to wince in pain.

"You ok," he asked with concern.

"Yea, I'm such a klutz I tripped and fell down the stairs yesterday," I said looking down and gave him my rehearsed statement.

"Did you go get looked at?"

"No, I'll be ok."

"Kaylen, you can hardly walk, let's go over to the Student Health building and get you looked at," he suggested, grabbing my books from me.

"I'm fine really. I just need to take some Tylenol and I'll be ok," I protested.

"For me, please. I just wanna make sure you're ok."

His eyes were full of concern, and I hesitantly agreed as we headed towards the student health building. I was seen immediately, and after a few X rays, the doctor told me that I had four fractured ribs as well as some bruising.

"You wanna tell me how this happened," Doctor Lynn asked me.

"I fell down some stairs," I softly replied while looking down.

"You sure about that," she asked skeptically.

I simply nodded.

"Ok, well, I'm gonna wrap your abdomen and give you some 800mg ibuprofen for the pain."

She lifted my shirt to wrap me, and I heard her gasp. I held my head down, so she didn't see the silent tears rolling down my face.

"You know Kaylen, I used to fall down the stairs a lot too when I was your age. Those stairs almost killed me one day, and it was then that I realized stairs aren't supposed to hurt you," she said softly as she started to wrap my abdomen. "My door is always open, Kaylen, anytime you wanna talk about those stairs, just let me know. As a matter of fact, here is my number. You can call me anytime; day or night." She placed her card in my hands. "I'm recommending that you don't come to class for the rest of the week, you need to let your body rest and allow your ribs to heal."

"I can't miss class," I frantically replied.

"Ok, well how about we do this, I have a cot in my office, and you can come in here for the rest of the week. I'll get all your assignments, and you can complete them while you're here resting, how does that sound?"

"Ok," I replied as I stood to leave. "Thank you."
She smiled.

"I'll see you in the morning, Kaylen," she said, and I walked out of the room to find Julian sitting in the waiting room.

"Hey, how you feeling," he asked as I made my way towards him.

"A little better," I answered softly as we headed out the door.

"You need me to walk you to class?"

"I'm not going to class today. I have to get my prescription filled."

"Well, I don't have any more classes for today, how about I take you?" He suggested.

"I don't wanna burden you."

"It's no problem, really," he insisted, and I agreed to let him take me.

We walked in silence to his car. I was lost in my own

thoughts. He hit the remote on his 2001 BMW and opened the door for me before walking around to the driver's side and got in.

"You have a specific place you get your medicine from?"

I shook my head no.

"Ok, well, there's a CVS not too far from here."

We rode in silence and listened to the radio.

"This is your boy Brian Dawson, here's a classic from my girl Eve, keep it locked on K97.5," the radio announcer said just as *Love Is Blind* played on the radio.

"Love is blind and it'll take over your mind

Cause what you think is love it's truly not

You need to elevate and find..."

The words of the song touched something in me, and I turned my head to look out the window as tears rolled down my face. It was almost as if Eve wrote this song especially for me. Julian turned down the radio and asked if I was ok.

"I'm fine," I replied quietly while I wiped my tears quickly so he couldn't see them.

"I'm a good listener, Kaylen. Anytime you want to talk, I'm here for you," he said as he grabbed my hand and lightly squeezed it.

"You don't even know me," I responded more harshly than I intended.

"True, but I'm a firm believer that God puts people in your life for a reason."

I began to wonder what God's purpose for putting Black into my life was. It was obvious that God just didn't like me; why else would I be going through this? But I keep forgetting, this is what love is, right?

"Tell me about you, Kaylen," he said.

"There's not much to tell," I shrugged.

"Well, I'll tell you about me then. I'm 21, originally from Decatur, Georgia, I have two older brothers, my dad is a criminal defense lawyer and my mom is a pediatric doctor," he said.

"A real life Huxtable family."

"I guess you could say that," he smiled.

"Ok, well, I'm 18, born and raised in North Carolina, I'm an only child," I told him purposely leaving out my parents.

"What made you want to study psychology," he asked.

"I don't know, I guess because I've always wanted to help people, and I've always been fascinated at how the mind works."

"Ok, so what made you wanna come to NCCU?"

"I've always wanted to go to an HBCU, and Central has a great psychology program."

"Same here and plus this is my dad's alma mater, so I always knew I would be an Eagle," he said proudly.

"You plan on doing any pledging," he asked as we turned into the CVS on Miami Blvd.

"I've always wanted to pledge Delta Sigma Theta, but I'm not sure I will." I said, knowing Black would never go for me pledging, hell he barely wanted me to go to school.

"I pledged Omega Psi Phi my freshman year, and it was the best thing I've done. I gained a lot of brothers in the process. I think you should pledge, it's a great experience, and you get to be around me being that deltas are sisters to the Omega's" he said as he smiled and caused me to giggle slightly.

"Maybe," I said shrugging.

"I'll run this in for you right quick," he said while grabbing my prescription and got out of the car.

As I leaned back in my seat, I began to think about my relationship with Black and how it changed so much from when I met him. Was it me? Was I doing something wrong? I began to question myself and my appearance. Maybe I could keep myself up a little better and then he would fall back in love with me.

I looked around the parking lot and noticed they had a bunch of different shops and eateries in the area. I looked to my left, and what I saw caused my heart to shatter. There was Black hugged up with another female leaving the Ruby Tuesday's that was next door.

CHAPTER SEVEN

I know y'all thinking, "I know she left him after she saw him with another woman".

The answer was no. Hell, I didn't even mention it to him. Instead, I walked around like everything was all good. That whole week I spent in the office with Doctor Lynn. Many times she tried to get me to open up, and every time I thought about it, I would hear mama's words, "What goes on in this house, stays in this house".

Black left for almost a week after my beating. When he returned he apologized and gave me a Teacup Yorkie I named "Jazzie". Of course I forgave him, and things were ok for a while. I was doing everything in my power not to make him angry. I kept the house clean, his food hot, laundry done, and I sexed him like my life depended on it.

Julian and I became closer. In fact, after every class he had, he would come and sit with me in the office. And the days he didn't have class, we would sit and talk, laugh, eat or study together. I found myself really liking him, but he was too nice, and I knew it wouldn't work. I would settle for being just his friend, though. After all, he was nothing like Black, and what Black gave me was really love, right?

"How are you feeling today, Kaylen?" Doctor Lynn asked me on my last day in her care.

"A whole lot better. I'm not in as much pain, and I'm starting to feel like my old self again," I told her as I gave her a small smile.

"That's great to hear, I'm gonna miss you next week though," she said.

"I'm not leaving school Doctor Lynn, you'll see me," I told her and giggled.

"I know that, I just got so used to you being here, that's all," she said as she sat down beside me. "You know, Kaylen, I never told you my story. Would you like to hear it?" She asked, and I nodded.

Before she could even begin, she was paged to the front.

"Looks like we're gonna have to take a rain check." She said, and I gathered my things after noticing four o'clock was approaching.

"That's ok, Doctor Lynn, I'm sure we'll get to it someday," I told her.

"I'll see you later, Kaylen," she said before walking out the door.

Walking across campus towards my car, I collided with a girl who wasn't paying attention to where she was going.

"I am so sorry," she said while bending down to pick up my books and papers.

"It's ok," I told her as I helped her gather my things.

"My mind is so boggled today, and I wasn't even paying attention to where I was going," she replied softly.

For some reason I was drawn to this girl, I know I should've been getting home, but my feet wouldn't move.

"I can relate. I'm Kaylen." I told her holding out my hand.

"Mya," she said as she shook my hand.

"It's nice to meet you, Mya, you new here?" I asked her.

"I just started back today, I've been out on maternity leave for six weeks. I just had a baby boy," she said and beamed with pride.

"Congratulations," I said and smiled back.

"Thank you," she replied.

"I don't have many friends, but I feel a connection with you. Maybe we can do lunch or something," I told her.

"That would be great!" She said, and we exchanged numbers.

"MYA!" A voice boomed from behind me causing us both to jump.

"I gotta go," she said frantically and rushed toward who I know to be Alonzo Tate, star running back here at NCCU.

I rushed to my car after noticing that it was after four thirty. I drove like a bat out of hell to get home in time. It was just my luck that there was an accident on NC 42, so traffic was backed up. I pulled out my phone and called Black.

"Where the fuck are you?" He barked not even bothering to say hello.

"There's an accident on 42, and traffic is backed up." I told him, my voice was trembling with fear.

"You got ten minutes to get to this fucking house," he said before he hung up on me.

I was twenty minutes away from my house, so I knew there was no way I'd make it in ten minutes.

I mentally and physically prepared myself for the knock down drag out that was sure to happen, my body trembled in fear. Almost an hour later, I pulled up to my house and saw Rico & Twon's cars in the driveway. I breathed a sigh of relief; surely he wouldn't beat me in front of them.

I entered the house, and I was greeted by marijuana smoke and loud music. No sooner than I reached the kitchen, Black was on me.

"Bitch, didn't I tell you ten minutes? That was an hour ago!" He shouted before backhanding me, and I dropped to the floor and held my face.

"I tried, Black, but the traffic was backed up," I told him that with tears in my eyes.

"You should've went another way," he said when he grabbed my hair.

"I'm sorry," I told him with tears rolling down my face.

My hair felt like it's been ripped from my scalp due to his tight grip.

"You gonna learn to do what I tell you, Kay," he said through clenched teeth and brought his free hand down on my face, and I felt my lip split.

Then he brought his size twelve boot down on my abdomen so hard, he literally knocked the wind out of me, and I felt liquid run down my legs. Another backhand to the face was followed by a fist to the eye, another fist to the jaw, and I swear I heard something crack. He hit me over and over again, almost in a blind rage.

I felt myself about to pass out from the pain and then I hear, "What the fuck you doing man?" Rico yelled and pulled Black off of me and pushed him back.

"This ain't yo business, Rico," Black said as he glared at Rico.

"Man, this is a female, fuck you hitting her like that for, nigga?" Rico replied angrily and kneeled down to check on me.

"Man, fuck that bitch, she need to learn to listen." Black spit harshly and charged back towards me, and Rico grabbed him and bear hugged him.

"Twon!" Rico yelled, and Twon came rushing into the kitchen.

"What the fuck!" Twon said looking at me and rushed to my side.

"Man, take this nigga somewhere for I kill him, I got her,

bruh." Rico said seriously and pushed Black toward Twon who pulled him outside screaming obscenities.

"Damn KK, I gotta get you to a hospital, mama," he said and gently picked me up from the floor.

Three hours later, I was sitting in a hospital bed with two black eyes, a broken jaw that had to be wired shut, along with blue and black bruises everywhere. He also re-injured the fractured ribs that were just beginning to heal. The doctor also informed me that I had a miscarriage. I didn't even know I was pregnant.

I was empty inside. I had lost my baby at the hands of Black. I was tired, y'all. There I was only eighteen year's old and living in hell with the devil himself. I didn't want to live like that anymore, but what could I have done? I didn't have a job or any money at the time; Black took care of me. I couldn't leave.

Rico stayed with me the whole time I was in the hospital. The only time he left my side was to go home and change clothes or check on his spots.

"KK, you gotta leave that nigga, ma. He would've killed you if we wouldn't have been there," Rico said sincerely as tears rolled down my face. "My sister almost lost her life behind a nigga like him. That ain't love, lil mama," he said and grabbed my hand and caressed it with his thumb. "I'll help you get away from him, if that's what you want, but you gotta want it, KK. I can talk until I'm blue in the face, but if you ain't trying to leave then I'll be wasting my breath." He said while he wiped my tears. "Just think about it. I'll be back later, ok?" He said, and I nodded as he kissed my forehead and walked out of the room.

Could I really leave and been happy without Black? How would I survive without him? I loved him with all of me; I couldn't just walk away. He beat me because he loved me, right? Wasn't that love?

CHAPTER EIGHT

They kept me in the hospital for four days. I had Rico go up to my school and get my assignments. He also let them know I was in the hospital. I was so grateful for Rico. In those four days he literally became my best friend and shoulder to cry on. Kapri never called or came to see me once, even after I had Rico call her to tell her what happened.

"That nigga, Black, going crazy cause I won't tell him where you at," Rico said as I motioned with my hands for a pen and paper.

What am I gonna do? I wrote.

"You gotta leave, ma. If you don't, that nigga gone fuck around and kill you," Rico said softly.

Where am I gonna go, I don't have any family here other than my daddy, and I don't wanna go there, I wrote.

"Come stay with me, I have three extra rooms at my house. Let me help you, KK," he said grabbing my hand.

Why are you helping me? Black is your friend, I wrote.

"Don't get it twisted, mama. Black and I are far from friends. I deal with him off the strength of Twon. I'm helping you because you remind me so much of my sister. She was in a situation like yours, and we didn't know it. I wished somebody helped her like I'm helping you. Dude used to beat her ass on the regular, and when she tried to leave, he almost killed her. Somebody putting they hands on you ain't love, KK. Love ain't supposed to hurt," he said as he gripped my hand and looked in my eyes.

This is the only kind of love I know. I watched my father beat my mother my whole life. I thought this is what love was all about, I wrote with tears rolling down my face.

He got out of his chair and sat on the bed beside me. Rico wrapped me in his arms and allowed me to cry on his chest.

"KK, any nigga that put his hands on a female is a coward, you father included. Love should never be a black eye or a busted lip. If you're ready KK, I can help you, but you gotta be ready, ma." He said rubbing my back as I continued to cry.

He'll find me here, I gotta leave, I wrote.

"That nigga ain't gone fuck with you as long as you with me, I promise you that." Rico said, and I saw his jaw tighten.

How can you be so sure? I wrote.

"Because he knows I won't hesitate to put a bullet in his ass. Besides, I'm his boss, he ain't dumb enough to bite the hand that's feeding him," Rico said. "But if you insist on leaving, my sister, Sherika, lives in Georgia. I could drive you down there, and she'll help you. She was in your shoes six years ago," he said as he looked at me.

We sat in silence as I contemplated what I was gonna do. A part of me wanted to stay, and a part of me wanted to leave. I was tore up, because even though I hated what he did to me, I was still very much in love with Black.

I was being discharged the next day, so I had to make a quick decision. Going with my first mind I wrote, *Let's do it.*

"You serious, KK?" He asked as he looked into my eyes, and I nodded.

He hugged me as tight as my injuries would allow.

My things, I wrote.

"Don't worry about that, Black is going down to Charlotte Friday, and we can get your things then if you want them. In the meantime, you can crash at my crib," he said.

And Kapri? I wrote.

"Relax mama, that's a thing of the past, and besides, we were never together in a relationship anyway, so she never came to my crib," he said shrugging.

What about school? I wrote.

"I'll call Sherika and have her find schools down there that have a good psychology program, but in the meantime, I'll see if you can do online classes or something." He said, and I nodded before I laid back on his chest.

Calm came over me. I felt safe with Rico, and I was finally

escaping Black. But I was still torn though because I was in love with him. And fleeing to Atlanta might have been the best thing for me at the time. The question was though, would I stay away?

CHAPTER NINE

After I was discharged, as promised Rico took me to his house in Knightdale. His house was an amazing four bedroom, three bathroom mini mansion.

"Come on, and I'll take you on a tour," Rico said grabbing my hand.

The living room was decorated in all white with gold trim. He let me know that, that room was just for show nobody ever sat in there. Next, he showed me the den, which was decorated in black and white. It kinda had a Scarface theme. His house kind of reminded me of Tommy's house in the movie Belly.

Next, he showed me the huge kitchen with granite counter tops and cherry oak cabinets. The backyard was HUGE with a Jacuzzi and swimming pool. He then took me upstairs and showed me the room I would be staying in as well as his own.

His room was amazing, he had a tall king size sleigh bed that had a ladder attached for you to climb up. He had white carpet throughout and beautiful mahogany antique dressers. His room was decorated in black and white. It had a relaxing vibe to it.

"I gotta run out for a minute, but make yourself at home, and I'll see you when I get back." Rico said and kissed my forehead before he left out.

I still wasn't able to talk, so I just gave him a nod. Once Rico was gone, I powered my phone on to see one hundred and thirty missed calls, seventy text messages and a full voice mailbox. I had a few missed calls from my mom, Kapri and Doctor Lynn. The rest were from Black.

I then checked my text messages.

BLACK: Baby I'm sorry, where are you?

BLACK: I'm going crazy without you Kay, I swear it won't happen again ma.

BLACK: You gon make me fuck you up Kay

BLACK: Bring yo ass home bitch

BLACK: I'm sorry baby, It won't happen again

BLACK: You gon be sorry when I find your stupid ass

The rest of the messages were basically the same. He went from apologizing to threatening me. I deleted all messages from him and checked the rest.

KAPRI: Girl where are you?! Black has been blowing my phone up like crazy! He said he's sorry for what he did and it won't happen again. Go home to your man and stop acting like a little girl! Damn, you act like he killed you! A man don't love you unless he beats you, don't you know that! Call me back!

After reading that message, I deleted all the other messages I had from Kapri. I didn't even bother listening to the voicemails from Black or Kapri, so I deleted them and moved on to the other ones.

"Hey Baby, it's mom. I haven't heard from you, call me and let me know you're ok. Love you."

"Hey Kaylen, it's Doctor Lynn, Julian tells me you haven't been to class. Hope everything is ok. Give me a call back."

"Hi Kaylen, this is Mya. I didn't know who else to call, I need your help. Call me or text me when you get this message."

After hearing the message from Mya, I immediately sent her a text.

ME: Hey, I just got your message. Are you ok?

MYA: No, I'm scared Kaylen and I don't know what to do. Alonzo beat me up pretty bad last night and I gotta get out of here.

ME: Where are you now?

MYA: I'm home, he took my car keys along with my purse and left me in the house so I can't leave.

ME: Is he there?

MYA: No, he left about thirty minutes ago for practice.

ME: Send me your address and I'm gonna have my friend come get you and bring you here.

MYA: Thank you so much Kaylen. 3033 Bryn Athyn Way Raleigh 27615

ME: I'll text you and let you know when he's on the way.

I immediately sent a text to Rico.

ME: Are you busy?

RICO: Never too busy for you, you ok?

ME: I need a favor, are you close to home?

RICO: Be there in 15

I placed my phone down and said a prayer to God for him to keep Mya safe until Rico got there. I knew there was a reason I was drawn to Mya, it's because she was me. I recognized the look of fear in her eyes when Alonzo called her name the other day because it reflected my own whenever Black was around.

I went downstairs and sat on the couch as I waited for Rico's arrival. Ten minutes had passed when he walked through the door.

"What's up KK?" He asked and kissed my forehead and sat next to me.

I grabbed the pen and paper and wrote down everything Mya said over the phone and threw in the fact that she has a newborn baby. After much thought, Rico agreed to help her.

"I'm doing this for you, KK, let her know I'm on my way," he said and walked out the door.

I texted Mya to let her know Rico was on the way and for her to be on the lookout for a dark blue Range Rover. I then went into the kitchen in search of something to cook for dinner. I searched the freezer and found a pack of chicken wings and decided to fry them up.

I sat them in a sink of hot water and headed upstairs and took a much needed shower while the chicken thawed out. After a thirty-minute shower, I threw on a pair of Rico's ball shorts and one of his t-shirts before I headed back downstairs.

I fixed Rico and Mya a delicious meal that consisted of fried chicken wings, mashed potatoes with homemade gravy, corn and biscuits. I made a smoothie for myself since I couldn't eat whole foods. Just as I was taking the biscuits out of the oven I heard the door open, seconds later Rico entered the kitchen with a baby carrier and Mya not too far behind.

"I see you done just made yourself at home," Rico said jokingly as he walked into the kitchen and nodded toward his clothes that I was wearing.

I jokingly rolled my eyes while I smiled as he made his way toward me.

"Damn KK, it smell good as hell in here," Rico said as he kissed my forehead before he sat the baby on the counter and reached for a chicken wing.

I popped him, nodding towards the sink for him to wash his hands.

"Hey Kaylen," Mya said quietly with her head down.

I walked up to her and pulled her into my embrace, and she broke down. I gently rubbed her back allowing her to get it out.

"I'm sorry," she said as she stepped back and wiped her tears.

I lifted her face. I saw she had a black eye and bruises all over her face along with scratches all over her neck. I motioned for her to wash her hands, so she could eat. I unbuckled the car seat and gently removed the handsome baby boy and cradled him in my arms. Tears fell from my eyes as I thought about my own baby and if it would've been a boy or girl.

Black took away my first opportunity to become a mother. I couldn't go back to him, could I?

CHAPTER TEN

It had been a whole month since my incident with Black, and I was finally able to talk since I had my wires removed the day before. I still stayed with Rico along with Mya and little Alonzo, whom we called AJ. I was speaking with Julian and Doctor Lynn via text. I was able to do a lot of my schoolwork online, so I was grateful for that.

The doctor cleared me to return to school, and I decided to stay with Rico instead of moving to Georgia like I had originally planned.

"Are you sure you're up to going to school tomorrow?" Rico asked when we sat on the couch and watched a movie with his head in my lap.

"Yea, it's time, and besides I can't hide from Black forever," I told him.

I had grown quite fond of Rico since I'd been there. In fact, I started looking at him in a whole new light. It was like I was seeing him for the first time and liked what I saw. Rico stood at 5'11", 210lbs, light brown skin, with slanted dark brown eyes, a Caesar cut and the longest eyelashes I ever saw on a man. He also had a deep dimple on the top of his left cheek that was absolutely adorable.

"You ain't gotta hide from that nigga, KK, I would never let anything happen to you," he said as he looked into my eyes.

For a while we just stared at each other and just as he leaned up to meet my lips with his own, Mya walked into the room.

"What y'all doing?" She asked as she sat on the couch with AJ in her lap, and I immediately reached for him.

"Nothing, watching Scarface," I told her as she handed me the baby, and I sat him on Rico's chest just as he flashed me a toothless grin that melted my heart.

"I kinda want to talk to you guys about something," she said nervously.

"What's up?" Rico asked.

"I want you guys to be his godparents," she blurted out.

"Really?" I said surprised, and I could see the shock on Rico's face too.

"Yea, I mean y'all are the closest thing to friends I have. Rico, you opened up your home to us, and you didn't have to, for that I will be forever grateful. Kaylen, you didn't think twice about helping me when I was in trouble. Over these few weeks you have become the sister I never thought I wanted. I love you guys," Mya said with tears in her eyes.

"Awwww girl, we love you too," I told her with tears welling in my own eyes as I motioned for Rico to sit up and handed him the baby.

I walked over to Mya, and we embraced and cried together.

"Come on little man, let's get up out of here, it's too much damn estrogen up in here," Rico said as he got up and walked out with AJ, which caused us to laugh.

"Kaylen, I kinda got something else to talk to you about," she said as she looked down.

"Ok," I said with a raised eyebrow.

"I'm going back home," She said and shocked the hell out of me.

"Wait, what? Are you serious?" I asked her.

"AJ needs his father, Kay. Alonzo and I have been talking every day for the past two weeks. He informed me that he's been going to therapy to work on his issues. But to be honest, I miss him," she said quietly.

For a moment we just sat in silence. Black crossed my mind, and I had to admit that I missed him a lot. The love was definitely still there, but could he change? I had a good thing going here with Rico. I shouldn't go back, should I?

"He's coming to pick me up down the street in an hour," Mya said and snapped me out of my thoughts.

"Ummm, ok, well, I don't want you to leave, but if you feel it's best for you then do what you feel like you have to do," I told her and exited the room.

Was I angry with her? Yes, because I didn't want her to leave. But I was even angrier because she unknowingly caused me to think about Black.

I hadn't talked to Black since I had been there. I had ignored all of his texts and calls. But at that moment, I was longing for his voice, his touch, his attention, his love. As if it was fate, my phone rang, and it was Black. I struggled with myself on whether I should answer it or not.

Then just before the phone stopped ringing, "Hello?"

CHAPTER ELEVEN

Ok, ok, ok, I know what y'all thinking. Did I go back? Yes I did, because truthfully, I loved Black with my whole heart, and I missed my man. I didn't leave right away though. In fact, I stayed with Rico for another two weeks before I decided to go back home.

Now to say Rico was pissed would be the understatement of the century, he was livid! The night I told him I was leaving he stormed out of the house and hadn't returned when I left for school the next morning.

Now, my mind was telling me to leave Black alone for good and stay with Rico, but my heart was so in love with Black that all logical thinking went out the window. I mean, the heart wants what it wants, right? Black assured me that he would never hurt me again, and foolishly I believed him.

I went back home about a week before Thanksgiving, and Black welcomed me with open arms, never once questioning me about where I had been. That night Black catered to me, he fed me, bathed me, massaged my body and made love to me like he would never see me again!

All was well in our house, and I couldn't have been happier. I still hadn't heard from Rico even though I made numerous attempts to reach out to him. I was on cloud nine, so even he wasn't going to bring me down.

I had barely talked to Mya, and that bothered me a little because I hadn't seen her on campus either. I figured I would see her sooner or later, so I shrugged it off.

Now Kapri was a whole other story. As soon as I came back home, she magically appeared. She informed me that she was pregnant with her first child, and I wanted to be happy for her, I really did, but I just couldn't be. Something was different about her, and I couldn't put my finger on it, but something told me that our friendship would never be the same.

"Hey Doc," I said as I walked in Doctor Lynn's office.

"Hey Kay, how you doing?" She asked when she stood and embraced me.

"I'm good, I got a free period, so I decided to come see you," I said as I sat down in the chair in front of her desk.

"Well, lucky for you, I'm on lunch," She informed me and smiled. "What's been going on, Kay?"

Over the past few months I had grown extremely close to Doctor Lynn, so much that I shared everything with her, and she never once judged me. Even when I told her I was going back to

Black, she voiced her concerns, but she never judged. In a way, she became a confidante.

"Everything is great, Doc," I said. "It truly is. Black has been wonderful since I've been back home."

"I'm not happy with your decision to return to him Kaylen, but if that's where you want to be then nobody can stop you," she said.

"He's different this time, Doc. He's getting help, and things couldn't be better," I told her.

"Let me tell you a story," she said as she got up and sat down next to me. "When I was around your age, I met this guy named Omar. Chile, that man was some kind of fine! He swept me off of my feet, and we had a whirlwind romance. He asked me to marry him when I was just nineteen years old, and of course I said yes.

We had a wonderful marriage, until one day we got into a horrible argument. That was the very first time he hit me, and I blamed myself for making him so angry. After the first time, it became a routine thing. He beat me for any and everything. I left and ended up meeting this lady named Kerry. She was the manager for a place called Harbor Inc., a domestic violence shelter in Smithfield, North Carolina. I stayed for a few weeks and went back to Omar. Everything was good for a while and then the fighting started back up. Well one day, I got tired of being tired, and I decided to fight him back. That night he shot me four times and left me to die. Luckily, my phone was near me, and I was able to call for help before passing out. He shot me in the upper torso, hip, stomach and lower back. I was hospitalized for almost six months. I had to learn how to walk again. I was told that I would never be able to have children because of the damage done by the bullet to my stomach. I vowed to never allow another man to put his hands on me because that's not love.

When I met Derek, I wouldn't allow myself to fall in love with him even though he tried. It wasn't until I started to love myself that I realized that this man loved me wholeheartedly. I said that to say this, don't ever allow a man to have control over you to the point that you lose yourself. Love isn't pain, Kaylen. I see a lot of myself in you. Don't let what happened to me happen to you. Get out before it's too late." She said, and we both have tears in our eyes. "Here, I want you to have something, this poem got me through some tough days in my life," she said and handed me a poem entitled, "I Got Flowers Today" By Paulette Kelly.

I took the paper from her, I stuffed it into my bag and didn't give it a second thought, not knowing that it too would help me get through some tough obstacles.

"Ok Doc, I gotta go, see you later," I said and exited her office to head to my next class.

After my class load was finished, I headed home to meet my man. I was on cloud nine, y'all. My relationship was back to the way it was when I first met Black, and I loved it. Funny thing about being on cloud nine is you gotta come down at some point. Well, in my case, snatched down because that's exactly what happened.

The bullshit started back, and this time it was ten times worse than before. Brace yourself for what's about to come, because shortly after the New Year shit got too real!

CHAPTER TWELVE

Around the end of January, I noticed Black had picked back up on some of his bad habits. I was a little late getting home from school one day, and he threw a glass at the wall. Another time when Jazzie peed on the floor, and I didn't get it up fast enough, he cussed me out something terrible after punching a huge hole in the wall. He never hit me though, so it didn't bother me too much.

February 4th was a day that I would never forget. It was a regular Saturday, so I decided to perform my Saturday ritual of cleaning. I put my hair up in a messy ponytail, threw on a pair of velour short shorts and a blank tank top. I didn't put on any underwear because I was home and didn't feel the need to.

I turned on the surround sound, and Mary J's "Real Love" filled the house. I was in the front room vacuuming, and I bent down to pick up one of Black's controllers. I never realized that Black and Rico had entered the house.

"Kay, what the fuck man, go put on some fucking clothes!" Black screamed and scared the shit out of me because I hadn't heard him come in.

I turned around to find a snarling Black beside Rico whose face I couldn't read, but damn he looked good.

"Now!" Black yelled and caused me to jump.

I turned the vacuum off quickly and ran upstairs with my heart beating out of my chest.

"Calm down Kay, everything is going to be ok," I said to myself.

I heard the front door close, so I knew that Rico had left, and I counted in my head. Before I could even get to twenty, Black had stormed through the bedroom door with an evil look on his face.

"What the fuck was that shit, Kay? You want that nigga or something?" He asked as he walked toward me, and I took a step back.

"No Black, I didn't even hear y'all come in," I told him.

"Don't lie to me, Kaylen. You fucking that nigga?" He said and grabbed the front of my shirt and ripped it.

"I swear to you, baby," I told him and covered my breasts with my hands.

"The fuck you covering up for, huh?" He asked as he grabbed me by the throat and pushed me into the wall hard. "I see I'm gon have to teach you not to ever fuck with me," he said and fumbled with his belt with one hand while the other was around my neck.

Please, God, don't let him do what I think he's about to do, I said to myself just as he ripped my shorts and violently rammed himself into me. It literally felt like my vagina was on fire; in and out he went viciously as tears fell from my eyes.

"You see what you make me do, Kay," he said in my ear as he continued to violate me.

I stared absently at the wall ahead as he forced himself in and out of my tunnel. I felt his body stiffen, and seconds later I felt him ejaculate inside me.

"Go get cleaned up and fix me something to eat," he said as he pulled out of me and let me go.

I was almost like a zombie as I did everything he told me to do. Mentally, I was somewhere else though.

"He just raped me," I said to myself in a whisper as tears fell rapidly from my eyes.

I got in the shower and literally scrubbed my skin until it turned red, I felt so dirty, so filthy.

Did I leave Black after that? Nope. I didn't even blame him for what he did to me; I blamed myself. If I hadn't been wearing what I was wearing it never would've happened.

Crazy right?

CHAPTER THIRTEEN

From that day forward, Black just stopped caring about me and how I felt. He raped me at least three times a week, and I just laid there and stared off into the distance until he finished.

I know you're thinking, "Why did you stay?"

The answer is simple, I had lost myself in Black, and I loved him more than life itself.

Whenever Rico called or texted me I wouldn't answer, I felt like I was getting what I deserved because I came back. I begin to distance myself from Doctor Lynn, Julian and even Mya. I had even stopped going to class on a regular basis. I was embarrassed, ashamed and living in hell on earth.

Black's disrespect towards me got worse every day, and it got to the point where I didn't even want to live anymore. The funny thing about that is, if God is not ready for you then whatever you try to do to yourself won't work.

March 19th was the first time I tried to take my life. I

remember it very vividly. Black had just finished having his way with me and had left the house. I lay on the bed almost in a daze, just not wanting to live anymore. I slowly got up and went into the bathroom, opened the medicine cabinet only to find it empty.

I walked downstairs almost like a zombie. I went into the kitchen and retrieved the sharpest knife I could find. Slumping down the wall and onto the floor, I didn't even wince as I slit one wrist followed by the other. It didn't take long for the blood to start flowing, then darkness engulfed me, and I welcomed it. I was finally free. But imagine my surprise when I woke up in the hospital with Rico at my side. Once he noticed I was awake, he rushed to my side.

"Damn KK, you scared me, mama," He said as he looked into my eyes.

"What happened, why am I still here?" I asked hoarsely.

He went on to explain that he came by the house to meet Black. Once he saw that Black wasn't there, he started to leave, but something wouldn't let him. He knocked and rang the doorbell but got no answer even though my car was there, so he went around to the side door. He caught a glimpse of me and the blood all over the floor and immediately called 911. He then kicked the door in and attempted to wake me. I was unconscious at that point, and he didn't know what to do. Luckily, the paramedics arrived when they did.

"Why did you save me?" I asked him as tears rolled down

my face.

"You got too much to live for, mama," he said softly and caressed my cheek.

"I don't wanna live, Rico, life is too hard," I told him and sobbed.

"Listen to me, KK, don't say that shit again, you gotta fight, mama! There is a reason I showed up to your house when I did. There is a reason you're still here. It ain't your time mama, you got a whole life to live," He said and pulled me into his arms, and before I could respond the doctor walked into the room.

"Hey, Miss Gibson, I'm Doctor Snead, how are you feeling?" He asked me.

"Alive," I said so sarcastically it caused him to chuckle lightly.

"You're a very lucky lady, Miss Gibson. Had your friend not come when he did, you wouldn't be here right now. I don't know what you're going through, but it's not worth your life. Luckily the blood loss didn't affect the baby," he said.

"What baby?" I asked in shock.

"According to my chart, you're about six weeks pregnant," he said. "Now, due to the seriousness of your injuries, I'm gonna have to take you down to the mental health floor, and you'll be on suicide watch for the next seventy-two hours," he said.

"Is that really necessary, doc? She can come home with me," Rico said.

"I'm sorry son, but that's hospital policy with all suicide

patients, my hands are tied. You have any questions for me?" He asked, and we shook our head no. "Ok, well, you'll be transferred first thing in the morning," he said before he walked out of the room.

I sat back on the bed on the verge of tears when Rico pulled me into his arms.

"It's gonna be ok, mama. I'm here with you every step of the way," he said.

"What am I gonna do with a baby, Rico?" I asked him.

"We gonna get through this together, mama, but one thing I do know is that you gotta leave Black. I've already called Sherika, and she is expecting you in the next few weeks," He said in a voice that let me know it wasn't up for discussion, so I only nodded.

Why was God keeping me alive?? I didn't want to live anymore; life was too hard. I was only nineteen, is this is how my life is supposed to be? Now, I was having my own child. What am I going do now?

CHAPTER FOURTEEN

They kept me in the hospital for over a week, and Rico was with me every step of the way. I hadn't seen or heard from Black the whole time I was there. The nigga didn't even send a balloon or flowers. As soon as I left the hospital, I went to Rico's house, where I stayed until the first of April.

April 3rd at 3am, I arrived in Marietta, Georgia. Can you believe it? I was finally free from Black! I didn't tell anybody I was leaving. Hell, I didn't even take anything except Jazzie. Rico took care of my school transfer and enrolled me in Spelman College. I literally owed Rico my life. I was forever grateful to him and all that he did for me.

"I can't believe I'm free," I mumbled softly as we pulled up to the Hilton Atlanta.

"What you say, KK?" Rico asked me.

"I said, I can't believe I'm free."

"Well, believe it, mama. Besides, you got somebody else to

live for now," he said as he got out of the truck and went into the hotel.

After checking in, Rico and I went into our two bedroom suite where I took a much needed shower. After I put on my PJs, I went and said good night to Rico.

"Knock, knock," I said before I entered his room, and I was momentarily stopped in my tracks.

Rico was sitting on the edge of the bed in nothing but basketball shorts, and for the first time I noticed all his tattoos. Unconsciously I bit my bottom lip as my eyes roamed his toned body.

"I think you're supposed to wait for somebody to said come in before you just walk in, KK," he said, and he smirked and snapped me out of my thoughts.

"Sorry, I just wanted to said good night," I said softly before I put my head down.

In what seemed like a flash, Rico was standing before me and lifted my chin.

"What I tell you about holding your head down, KK?" He asked and looked into my eyes.

"Sorry," I said softly.

"Stop apologizing mama, you ain't did nothing wrong," he said before he softly kissed my forehead. "Get you some rest, KK, I'll see you in the morning," he said, and I turned to head back to my room.

As I was lying in bed, I said a silent prayer, and I was sleep within a matter of seconds. After six hours on the road, I was exhausted. A nightmare of Black standing over me with a dead baby in his arms covered in blood jolted me out of my sleep, and I woke up in a cold sweat.

"KK, you aight? I heard you screaming," Rico said as he rushed into my room.

"I had a nightmare," I said softly as tears welled up in my eyes.

"Come on, you can sleep with me," Rico said and reached for me.

"I wanna change first, my clothes are soaking wet," I told him slightly embarrassed.

He agreed before he walked out of the room. After I took a quick shower, I slipped on a pair of boy shorts and a tank top then headed to Rico's room. He looked to be sleeping peacefully, and I was just about to leave back out when he swung the covers back. I climbed into the bed facing him and snuggled into his embrace.

Rico placed a soft kiss on my forehead before we both fell into a peaceful sleep. His chin rested on my head, and my head rested on his chest.

I was awakened to Jazzie licking my face and voices coming from the suite living room. I picked her up and headed into the living room. I was met by Rico and, who I assumed to be, his sister.

"Morning KK, how you sleep, mama?" Rico greeted me.

"I slept like a baby," I said while smiling at him.

"I wanna introduce you to my sister, Sherika," he said.

I put Jazzie down and held out my hand to shake hers, only to have her pull me into her embrace. I immediately felt a connection to her as she slightly rocked me from side to side.

"Nice to meet you, Kaylen," she said as she released me and gave me a warm smile.

Sherika was beautiful. She was about 5'7", smooth brown skin and had the most exotic hazel eyes I've ever seen. She was built like a model but with more curves, her hair was cut close and dyed a honey blonde. Usually I found close cuts on women masculine, but she was rocking the hell out of hers.

"Nice to meet you, too," I told her.

"We took the liberty of going to grab you some things. The bags are in your room," Rico said. "I know you're hungry, so go get dressed, and we'll go out and get some lunch."

"What time is it?" I asked him.

"A little after two," he replied.

"Wow, I can't believe I slept that long," I said.

"I figured you were tired, that's why I didn't wake you," he said.

"I guess I'll go get dressed," I said as I went to my room where I found bags everywhere.

I looked through the bags. I found undergarments from Victoria Secret, lotion, deodorant, body spray, earrings, True Religion jeans, maxi dresses, sandals, Jordan's and a whole lot of other things. I decided on a ripped True Religion jean jumper, a white baby doll tee underneath and the space jam Jordan's.

After I took care of my morning hygiene, I took a long shower. After I got out of the shower, I got dressed and brushed my hair up into a messy ponytail. I put on the gold hoop earrings, sprayed some Love Spell body spray and headed out to the living room.

Entering the room Rico looked at me and laughed, which caused me to self-consciously look at my outfit.

"What?" I asked

"I told Sherika yo ass was a tomboy, and nine times out of ten you would throw on some jeans with them J's," he said smirked.

"You think you know me?" I asked.

We all laughed and headed out to get something to eat. I already felt at home here, and Black was the furthest thing from my mind. Yeah, Georgia was just what I needed. But could I stay away? I still loved Black very much, and since I was having his child, what was I going do?

CHAPTER FIFTEEN

Rico spent the entire week with me in Georgia, took me around the city and showed me around with Sherika. I went to the Spelman campus, and I loved the people and energy I got from being there. Rico announced that he would be leaving that day, and I was devastated.

"Come on mama, stop all that crying. I'll be back before you know it," he said while he hugged me and wiped my tears.

I had grown so much closer to Rico since we left North Carolina. If I was being real with myself then, I would've admitted that I was falling for him. But he wouldn't have wanted me, would he?

"I know Rico, I'm just really gonna miss you, that's all," I said while I was sniffling and hugging him tight.

"You'll be ok, mama. Sherika is gonna take good care of you," he said.

"I know," I said softly.

"I gotta go, but you know that I'm only a phone call away, right?" He asked and looked into my eyes, and I nodded. "Ok, no more tears, this is a new beginning remember?" He said before he kissed my forehead, cheeks and the top of my nose then got in his truck and winked at me before pulling off.

I stood and watched him drive away until I could no longer see the taillights, then I turned and slowly entered Sherika's house. Upon entering the house, I found Sherika on the couch watching TV.

"Hey, I guess Rico is gone?" She asked as I sat down beside her.

"Yea, he just left," I told her softly.

"Well, don't look so sad, I mean, I'm not Rico, but I'm not that bad," she said as she jokingly bumped my shoulder and caused me to giggle.

"I'm just gonna miss him, that's all," I said as I stared at the TV.

"Kay, are you in love with Rico?" She asked me out of the blue.

"What, huh, no, uh why would you ask me that?" I stammered caught off guard.

"You can be honest with me, I can keep a secret," she whispered and winked at me.

"Rico and I are just friends, he helped me through some rough times, nothing more nothing less," I said slowly, not sure if I even believed that.

"Ummmm hmmm, ok," she said while looking at me with the side eye.

"Anyway, what's for dinner?" I asked her and changed the subject.

"I don't do too much cooking, so we can go out," she said.

"How about we hit the grocery store, and I'll cook." I said and shrugged.

"How about I take you out tonight, my treat of course, and you cook tomorrow night? Deal?" She asked and held out her pinky, and I grabbed it.

"Deal," I said and smiled at her.

"Just let me grab my purse, and we can go," she said and got up off the couch.

I ran upstairs to get my purse and phone and then I remembered Jazzie hadn't been out. I took her out back to let her do her thing, filled up her food and water bowl then I met Sherika in the living room.

"Ready," I said.

We headed out to the garage and jumped into her 2005 BMW 750i. I noticed another car beside hers was covered up.

·"You got another car?" I asked and turned to look at her.

"Uh uh, that's yours," she said nonchalantly, and my eyes bulged.

"You said what now?" I asked caught off guard.

"Rico didn't tell you?" She asked with a raised eyebrow.

"Oh my God, he bought me a car?" I asked in disbelief as I

got out of the car and ripped the car cover off.

There was a dark grey 2005 Honda Accord LX with tinted windows and 20 inch plated rims. I covered my mouth, and tears filled my eyes. I hurried and grabbed my phone to call Rico.

"Miss me already?" He said as he answered.

"You bought me a car," I squealed.

"You gonna need it to get around and back and forth to school," he said nonchalantly.

"Rico, this is too much, you gotta let me pay you back! How much did you pay for this car?" I asked him.

"That's none of your business, just think of it as an early birthday present," he said.

"You didn't have to do this for me, how can I ever repay you, Rico?" I said as I sobbed into the phone

"Uh uh, no more tears remember? And you don't owe me shit KK, I'm a real nigga, mama. I do shit because I want to, not because I have to. Just take care of yourself and be everything you can be, ma, and know that I'm always in your corner," he said.

"I love you, Rico, and I mean that. I don't know where I would be without you," I told him.

"I love you too, mama, now enjoy your car and call me later ok," he said.

"Ok."

"Oh yea, check the glove compartment, I left you a little something," he said and ended the call.

I opened the door, and I fell in love with the car some more, opened the glove compartment and found the title with my name on it and an envelope. I opened the envelope and found a bank statement with my name on it and a visa card. My eyes bulged at the amount.

"Ten thousand dollars!" I exclaimed, and I looked at it again, but the amount didn't change.

I looked at Sherika with tears streaming down my face as she smiled at me.

"You knew didn't you?" I asked her, and she nodded and got out of her car.

"Real niggas do real things. You drive," she said as she winked at me and tossed me the keys.

I put the key in the ignition, and it came to life. I backed out of the driveway, and we were off to dinner. Sherika directed me to Gladys Knight's Chicken and Waffles as we rode blasting Mary J. We entered the restaurant and were immediately seated. After placing our orders, we sat and make small talk.

"So, did you like your surprise?" She asked me and smiled.

"I feel like it's all a dream, I can't believe he did that for me," I said.

"Rico is a good person with a huge heart, but I gotta admit, even I was taken aback by all this, you must be pretty special," she said while smiling at me.

"I have to find a way to pay him back," I told her.

"He won't take it, trust me I know. Pay him back by being

everything you were meant to be in this life," she said when she grabbed my hand.

We were interrupted by the waiter bringing our food. My mouth watered at the sight of the fried chicken, mac & cheese, collards, yams, smothered pork chops and mashed potatoes. Yea I know, sounds like a lot, but I was hungry!

"That's gonna be a fat baby," Sherika said while eyeing my plate and laughing.

I joined her in the laughter and threw a napkin at her.

For the first time in my nineteen years on this earth, I felt young and free. I was in a new place with a new outlook on life. Did I still love Black? Absolutely, but until he got his act together, there could be no us.

CHAPTER SIXTEEN

Today was my first day at Spelman, and I could honestly say I loved it. The fact that it was an all-girl school was a plus for me. The commute wasn't as bad as I thought it would be. It only took me about twenty-five minutes. I'll admit though that I missed NCCU and the people I met there. My mind shifted to Dr. Lynn, and I made a mental note to call her as soon as I could.

I walked to my car after class, and I saw a girl with her baby, and it dawned on me that I hadn't even made an appointment. Pulling away from campus, I rode around a little bit trying to get to know the city. The ringing of my phone snapped me out of my thoughts.

"Hello?"

"Hey baby, now why haven't I heard from you?" My mother asked.

"Just had some things going on, but I was gonna call you soon," I said, happy to hear her voice.

"Things going on like what? Did that boy do something to you?" Mommy asked.

"I really don't wanna talk about it," I said softly.

"You know you can talk to me about anything, right?" She asked me.

"Yes ma'am I know, but I'm ok really, as a matter of fact, I'm not very far from you now," I told her.

"Ok, KK, and what do you mean by that? Like you're coming to visit?" She asked me in confusion.

"No mom, as in, I live in Georgia," I told her, and I had to take the phone away as she fussed.

"Kaylen Monaè Gibson are you telling me that you moved to the exact same state as your mother, and you haven't come to see me once?" she screamed.

"Calm down mom, I was gonna tell you as soon as I got settled," I told her.

"No, how about you should've told me when you decided to move," she said.

"I'm sorry, Mommy, I really was gonna tell you."

"What part of Georgia, Kaylen?" she asked.

"Marietta," I told her.

"Well, that's about three hours from me, so I expect a visit soon! Are you still in school?" She asked.

"Yes ma'am, I'm at Spelman," I said and smiled.

We talked for a few more minutes, and I promised to come down the following weekend. I pulled up to Sherika's, and I saw an unfamiliar car in the driveway. Walking into the door I was greeted by Jazzie, and I saw Sherika on the couch hugged up with a beautiful Spanish looking chick.

"Hey Kay, how was school?" Sherika asked looking up at me.

"It was great," I said smiling.

"Kay, I want you to meet my girlfriend, Rae. Rae meet Kaylen," she said, and it caught me off guard because I didn't even know she was a lesbian.

"Nice to meet you, Kaylen," Rae said and got up to shake my hand.

Rae was absolutely breathtaking! She stood at about 5'9", sun kissed skin, gorgeous green slanted eyes and a body to die for. She actually put me in the mind of Christina Milian.

"Same here, well, I'll get out of your way. I got a ton of homework," I said and turned to head upstairs. "Oh yea, Ree, I need to make an appointment with an OB," I said when I turned back around.

"Ok, I'll call my doctor in the morning and make you an appointment," She said, and I nodded before I headed upstairs to my room.

I started on my homework for my Research Methods class. I was about an hour in when I felt myself about to doze. I hopped off the bed and headed downstairs to make dinner. I walked past Sherika's room, and I heard cries of passion.

"Well, at least one of us is getting some," I said to myself as I walked down the stairs.

For dinner I decided on homemade meatloaf, mashed potatoes, string beans, homemade biscuits and for desert, banana pudding. Just as I was taking the banana pudding out of the oven, Sherika walked into the kitchen followed by Rae.

"Girl, you got it smelling right in here," Sherika said and pulled the plates and cups out of the cabinet.

"You're just in time, the food is ready," I told her.

We sat and enjoyed the wonderful meal that I prepared along with the delicious banana pudding.

"Girl, if you keep cooking like that, I'm gon need to hit the gym every day," Sherika said and rubbed her stomach as we sat in the living room stuffed.

"Forget that, I'm moving in if you cooking like that on the regular," Rae said, and we all laughed.

For the rest of the night we sat around talking, laughing and joking before I decided to call it a night. I entered my room and checked my phone to see a missed call from Rico, a missed call from my dad and a text from an unfamiliar number. I clicked on the message icon, a chill ran up my back at the message I read.

YOU STARTING TO MAKE ME ANGRY KAYLEN! WHERE THE FUCK YO STUPID ASS AT? WHEN I SEE YOU IM GONNA WHOOP YOUR ASS BITCH! I SWEAR IF YOU WITH ANOTHER NIGGA IM KILLING YOU AND HIM. SO FOR YOUR SAKE YOU BETTER SHOW YOUR SELF IN THE NEXT 24 HRS, BECAUSE IF I HAVE TO

FIND YOU IT AIN'T GONNA BE PRETTY! YOU BELONG TO ME BITCH, REMEMBER THAT!

My hands started to shake as I read the message, and I started to hyperventilate. What if he found me? What was I going do? I took deep breaths to calm myself down, and it dawned on me that he had no clue I was in Georgia, and I knew for damn sure Rico wasn't going volunteer that information. I breathed a sigh of relief, deleted the message and made a mental note to have my number changed.

CHAPTER SEVENTEEN

It was the middle of August, and I was officially six months pregnant and big as a damn house! Now I knew it was hot in North Carolina, but I'll be damned if it ain't sweltering in Georgia! I was sitting on the couch relaxing in the AC with Jazzie at my feet when I heard the door open, and I assumed it was Sherika.

"Hey Ree, my appointment is at 3:00 are you still going with me?" I asked not bothering to turn around.

"I wouldn't miss it for the world," I heard a smooth baritone voice say, and I turned around to see Rico smiling at me in all his sexiness.

"Ricooooooooooo!" I screamed and hopped up off the couch as fast as my big belly would allow and jumped into his arms.

"I take it that you missed me." He said and held me tight as I inhaled his curve cologne.

"Why haven't you been to see me?" I asked him while I

stepped out of his embrace and waddled back to the couch

"A lot of shit was happening, mama, and I couldn't leave," he said and sat beside me.

I hadn't seen Rico since he brought me here, but we talked and texted every day.

"What happened?" I asked him and propped my arms up on my stomach.

"Twon got knocked," he said and sighed.

"Oh no, when?" I asked in shock.

Twon had always been like a big brother to me. In fact, he was the only other person besides Rico, Mya and Doctor Lynn that knew I was in Georgia.

"Long story short, he got pulled over, and he was dirty, so he tried to run; led the cops on a chase and got caught. I got him a good ass attorney though, and he got him a five year plea deal, with good behavior, he'll be out in two," Rico said.

"I hate that happened to him," I said as my eyes filled with tears.

It seemed as though I was overly emotional with this pregnancy, everything made me cry.

"He good though, it could've been a lot worse and stop with the tears, cry baby," Rico said and wiped my eyes.

"Shut up, punk. You hungry?" I asked him.

"Yea, I got a taste for some soul food from The Beautiful," he said, and my mouth watered.

The Beautiful was a restaurant in Bankhead that sold that

grandma style home cooked soul food.

"Well, we can go there after my appointment," I said.

"I'm hungry now, so I'm gon swing by Steak and Shake before your appointment," he said.

"Oh yes, let's go!" I said excitedly.

"Come on, greedy ass," he said pulling me to my feet, and I punch him in his chest and caused him to laugh.

"I missed you, KK," he said.

"I missed you too, punk," I said and kissed his cheek, then we headed out the door.

We enjoyed the day together. We went to my appointment where Sherika and Rae met us. The baby was doing fine and was due November 10th. When asked if I wanted to know the sex, I declined because I wanted to be surprised. Sherika, Rae and Rico weren't too happy about that.

We had a great dinner with Rae and Sherika before we went our separate ways. After dinner, Rico took me to Dave and Busters where I had a blast! He then took me out to get ice cream. We didn't get back until around 10pm.

"Wake up KK, we here," Rico said as he nudged me awake.

"Damn, I didn't even realize I fell asleep," I said, yawning.

"Come on, sleepy head," Rico said, and helped out of the truck.

We entered a dark house because Sherika stayed over at Rae's. I headed straight up to my room to shower and got ready for bed. I put on my pajamas, which consisted of pajama shorts and a tank top that barely covered my belly. Entering my room, I found Rico in my bed flipping through the channels.

"Ummmm, well, make yourself comfortable in my bed, why don't ya." I said sarcastically while I climbed in next to him and snatched the remote.

"I already did, thanks," he said and snatched the remote back, and I rolled my eyes. "Yo, why you got on that little ass shirt KK?" He said, laughing.

"Don't talk about my shirt punk, I'm comfortable," I said and laughed with him.

"Whatever you say, Kay," he said as he flipped through the channels before settling on "Love and Basketball".

He pulled me close, and I laid my head on his chest, and he put his hand on my belly and caused the baby to kick.

"I don't think my baby likes you," I said giggling with my head on his chest and listened to the rhythm of his heartbeat.

"Whatever, KK, she loves me," he said while he rubbed my stomach.

"How you know it's a girl?" I asked sleepily with my eyes closed.

"Cause I know everything," he replied kissing my forehead as I fell into a peaceful sleep.

CHAPTER EIGHTEEN

Early the next morning I was awakened to Rico placing soft kisses all over my protruding baby bump.

"Morning, sleepy head," Rico said as he kissed my forehead.

"Morning," I said groggily and got up to use the bathroom and took care of my morning hygiene.

"KK, we need to go get things for the baby." Rico said walking into the bathroom while I brushed my teeth, and I nodded.

Rico continued to stand behind me as I finished my morning hygiene, silently watching me. We stared at each other in the mirror, even after I was done. Before either of us knew it, I spun around quickly and planted a kiss directly on his soft lips.

Realizing what I did, I quickly said to a stunned Rico, "I am so sorry, I don't know what came over me."

Rico didn't respond, instead he grabbed my face lightly with both hands and kissed me with so much passion my knees buckled. He wrapped his arms around my waist, and pulled me as close as my belly would allow, Rico slid his tongue in my mouth, and I hungrily accepted it.

"Mmmmmmm," I moaned into his mouth when suddenly Rico pulled back.

"Damn KK, what we doing, mama?" He asked looking into my eyes.

The sparkle in his eye as he looked at me made me weak. It was a look I'd never seen before.

"I don't know, Rico. I can't explain it, but I can't say I didn't enjoy it," I said looking up at him.

"You know that when we cross that line, that's it, you're mine. So if there is even a small amount of doubt in your mind, we can act like this never happened," He said seriously, and I took notice that he said when, not if.

"I'm so confused right now because I want to be with you, Rico. But another part of me still loves Black, as crazy as that may sound. I guess what I'm trying to say is, I don't wanna jump into something with you until all those feelings for Black are completely gone," I said looking into his eyes, and noticed the fire behind them every time I mentioned Black.

"I respect your honesty, KK, and even if this doesn't go past friendship, know that I'm always here for you and the baby. I don't like the idea of you someday going back to Black, but you're grown. Just don't let a chance at true love pass you by chasing after the illusion of what you think love is," Rico said before kissing the top of my nose and walked out of the bathroom.

I slowly processed everything Rico said while I turned on the shower. Could it be that Rico is my true love? He could have any woman he wanted. He couldn't possibly want me, could he? There was something about Rico that had me drawn to him. Nothing between us was forced. It just came naturally.

I stepped in the shower and allowed the water to beat down on my back as I took the time to think. I know it's crazy, but I just couldn't turn my feelings for Black off just like that. I knew I shouldn't, but a small part of me actually missed Black. But another part of me was ready to say fuck Black and start a new life with Rico.

One thing was for certain though; I refused to jump into another relationship while I still harbored these feelings for Black. I turned the shower off and wrapped a big fluffy towel around myself. Entering my bedroom, I found Rico stretched out on my now made bed, fully dressed.

"Took you long enough," he said taking his eyes off of the TV to look at me.

"Oh hush," I said and walked toward my dresser to grab underwear.

"I'll be downstairs, don't take all day," Rico said tapping my ass lightly and walked out of the room.

I shook my head because I couldn't help the smile that graced my face after the small display of affection. I slid on my underwear and walked toward my closet, I decided on a cute terry cloth short maternity romper I got from Pea In A Pod. I lotioned my whole body with cocoa butter, I slipped my clothes on and slid my slightly swollen feet into my gold Chanel sandals.

I put on my gold hoops and charm bracelet from Rico, I pulled my growing hair up into a ponytail, sprayed on some Haiku, and grabbed my purse and headed out of the room in search of Rico.

"You ready?" I asked Rico walking into the living room.

"Yea, let's roll!" Rico said turning the TV off and getting off the couch.

We locked up and headed to his truck. After helping me get into the truck, Rico hopped in and pulled off. Just as we were about to hop onto I-75S my phone rang.

"Hi Mommy," I answered smiling.

"Hey baby girl, your aunt and I are coming to Atlanta to go shopping today. I expect to see you," She said and I heard my aunt consigning in the background.

"What time are you guys gonna get here?" I asked excitedly ready to see my mom.

"This GPS thingy says we're about thirty minutes from Atlanta," she said.

"I'm actually out already, so I can come meet you," I told her.

"Ok baby, I'll call you when we get off of the highway," she said and I agreed before hanging up.

"Which mall we going to Rico?" I asked Rico.

"Probably Cumberland, Phipps Plaza and then Lenox," Rico said.

"Well dang, somebody trying to spend a lot of money today," I said jokingly.

"I'm making sure my baby girl have everything she needs," Rico said.

"Why are you so adamant about this being a girl?" I asked him.

"Because I know everything," he said winking at me.

"Wanna put something on it?" I asked with a raised eyebrow while smirking.

"Bet it up," he said.

"One hundred dollars," I said.

"Make it two," He said holding out his hand, and I shook it.

Just as we pulled up to the mall, my mom called me back, and I directed her to the mall. Thirty minutes later, I saw my Aunt Carol's black Nissan Altima pull into the parking lot. I quickly hopped out of the car and flagged them down. They parked and got out. I quickly rushed into my mother's arms, tears filled her eyes as she rubbed my baby bump.

"My baby's having a baby," she cried.

"You always so damn dramatic, Karen," Aunt Carol said, shaking her head and pulled me into a hug.

"I missed you guys," I said smiling.

"Hmph, I can't tell. You've been in Georgia for four months, and we ain't seen your ass," Aunt Carol fussed.

"Sorry about that Auntie, it's been a lot going on," I said.

"Mmmm hmmm," she said.

"Mom, Aunt Carol, I want you to meet my friend Rico," I said as Rico approached.

"Nice to meet you ladies," Rico said politely.

"Well hell, now, I know why we ain't seen yo ass, you got this fine ass man with you. But I ain't mad at you niecey, cause baby is a work of art," Aunt Carol said and I was immediately embarrassed.

Aunt Carol was Mommy's youngest sister and always said whatever came to her mind.

"Carol, you need a filter on that mouth," Mommy said and caused us to laugh.

We entered the mall and hit store after store. Rico had to take several trips to the car during our shopping extravaganza. I bought a lot of neutral colors, you know, like green or yellow. Rico, who was so adamant about it being a girl, bought pink everything, along with Mommy and Aunt Carol, who seemed to agree with Rico.

After leaving the mall, Mommy and Aunt Carol followed us to a cute little baby boutique on the north side of Atlanta. Rico and I picked out a crib, dresser, rocking chair and a whole bunch of other things. By the time it was all said and done, Rico had spent a grand total of $9,387.65 on the baby without even blinking an eye.

We decided to go to eat, and during dinner Rico got up and

went to the bathroom. Mommy and Aunt Carol take that moment to grill me.

"You sure y'all just friends, Kay?" Mommy asked me.

"Yes Mom," I replied.

"That's what your mouth said, but them eyes are telling the truth, and you in love with that boy," Aunt Carol said.

"I see it in his eyes too, Kay," Mommy said smiling.

"We're just friends," I said again.

"Yeah ok, just friends my ass," Aunt Carol said.

"Well, I like him, I get a good vibe from him," Mommy said winking at me.

"He's a good person," I said smiling while thinking of all that Rico had done for me.

"Yes, he is, and that's gonna be my son in law," Mommy said, and before I could respond, Rico approached.

After dinner, we said our goodbyes to my mom and aunt, then headed home. I silently thought about everything my mom and aunt said. Could Rico be my future?

CHAPTER NINETEEN

Rico decided to stay in Georgia for a little while, and I was glad he did because on September 6th, 2006 my world came crashing down. I was lying on the couch with my swollen feet in Rico's lap as he gave me one of the best foot massages I'd ever had when my phone rung.

"Hello?"

"He's gone, baby," I heard my mother cry.

"Mommy, what's wrong, who's gone?" I asked her, now sitting up.

"Your father, he's, oh Lord help me," she said before dropping the phone and releasing a pained cry.

"Mommy!!" I screamed as tears rolled down my face.

"Kaylen, baby, this is Aunt Carol, I'm so sorry, baby," she said.

"What happened to him Auntie?" I asked her through my tears.

She explained that Daddy was doing a routine traffic stop, when he got out and approached the driver. The guy opened fire striking Daddy in the neck and chest. He was pronounced dead at the scene.

At this point, I dropped my phone and let out a guttural scream. My daddy had his faults, but I still loved him despite of it all. Now he was gone, and there wasn't anything I could do about it. Rico rushed to my side and grabbed my phone as Aunt Carol explained to him what was going on.

After hanging up with her, Rico pulled me into his arms and rocked me gently while rubbing my back as I cried. I suddenly sat up and looked at Rico through tear filled eyes.

"I gotta get to my mother!"

"We can leave right now if you want," he said and I agreed.

Racing upstairs I packed a few clothes, grabbed Jazzie and my purse then met Rico back downstairs. Just as we were about to walk out the door, Sherika and Rae came in.

"Hey y'all, where y'all going?" Rae asked.

One look at my puffy eyes and swollen face, Sherika rushed to me, and pulled me into her arms.

"What happened?" She asked Rico.

"Her pops got killed," he said softly causing me to break down all over again.

"Her mom is in Augusta, so that's where we're headed," he added.

"Give me a minute to pack some things, I'm coming with

you," Sherika said headed for the steps.

"Pack me a bag too babe," Rae said with tears in her eyes while pulling me into her arms.

"You guys don't have to do that," I said.

"This isn't up for discussion, you need support, and we're going, end of discussion," Rae said rocking me gently in her arms.

Thirty minutes later, we all piled into Rico's truck and hit the highway. Sherika held me the entire time as I cried softly the first half of the trip. Halfway there I informed Rico that I had to use the bathroom, and we stopped.

After using the bathroom and buying some water we exited, I hopped in the front seat this time, so I could direct Rico to Aunt Carol's house.

"You ok mama?" Rico asked me holding my hand.

"No, but I have to be strong for my mom," I said softly, looking out the window.

"You know I'm here for you, right?" He asked, and I nodded, giving him a slight smile.

"So are we," Rae and Sherika said in unison, causing me to lightly giggle.

An hour later, we pulled up to Aunt Carol's house. We got out of the car and headed up to the door just as Aunt Carol opened it. She pulled me into her arms and she hugged me tightly.

"I'm so sorry baby," she said softly. I nodded. "Your mom is upstairs lying down, I had to give her a mild sedative to calm her down," she said ushering us into the house.

I headed upstairs and found my mother curled up with a picture of Daddy, fast asleep. I placed a kiss on her cheek, and left her to rest. Heading back downstairs, I saw everyone sitting in the living room.

"Y'all hungry?" Aunt Carol asked as I took a seat next to Rico, and put my head on his shoulder.

"Yes," we all said in unison.

"Well, I'll whip something up right fast," she said getting up and headed for the kitchen.

"You don't have to do that Auntie, plus, I got a serious craving for Chinese," I said rubbing my belly.

"There's a really good Chinese restaurant not very far from here, let me get the menu," she said.

After getting the menu, we all looked over it and decided what we wanted then placed our orders.

"I'll go and pick up the food," Rico volunteered

"I'll come with you," Aunt Carol said and she and Rico headed out.

Rae, Sherika and I sat around talking as we waited on Aunt Carol and Rico to come back. In the middle of our conversation, Mommy came down the stairs. I rushed to her as she collapsed into my arms with tears streaming down her face.

"He can't be gone," she repeated over and over again as Sherika rushed over to help me carry her over to the couch.

For at least ten minutes, we cried together.

"Your father had his faults, but he didn't deserve to die like that," Mommy said, wiping her eyes.

"It's going to be ok, Mom," I said, rubbing her back as tears filled my eyes.

"He called me," she said, staring into space.

"Who Daddy, When?" I asked her

"The same morning he was killed, we argued, he wanted me to come home and I said no. I told him I didn't want to hear from him again unless he was signing the divorce papers," she said, with tears streaming down her face.

"It's not your fault mom, sometimes things happen that we have no control over. What happened to daddy is nobody's fault but the bastard who shot him" I said

"I know, baby," she said, lightly smiling and patting my hand just as Aunt Carol and Rico came through the door.

"Hey, Ms. Karen, I'm so sorry for your loss," Rico said.

"Thank you baby, I hope y'all brought me something to eat," she said smiling.

"Of course we did," Rico said, returning the smile.

For the rest of the night, we sat up and talked; reminiscing about all the good times we shared with Daddy and even a few of the bad. We decided to call it a night around 3am, and I climbed into bed with my mother, and we fell into a peaceful sleep.

CHAPTER TWENTY

The next two days were spent talking to Daddy's family, writing the obituary, having his body transferred to the funeral home, deciding on a suit for him to wear, a day to have the funeral along with everything else. Being that Mommy and Daddy were still legally married and I was his only child, all decisions were left up to us. We decided to bury Daddy on the following Saturday, so we were headed back to North Carolina that Wednesday.

I was extremely grateful for Rico, Rae and Sherika, they were such a big help to us and even volunteered to travel back with us. Early Wednesday morning around 7am, we hopped on the road headed for North Carolina. Mommy and I rode with Rico, while Rae and Sherika drove down with Aunt Carol. Three stops and seven hours later, we arrived at the home I grew up in, the home I hadn't stepped foot into since the day I moved out.

Mommy was overcome with emotion as soon as we pulled up

in the driveway and saw the wreath on the door. Daddy's burgundy Dodge Ram sat parked in the driveway. We all filed out of the car and entered the house. Looking around, I noticed that Daddy hadn't changed a thing. Our family pictures lined the wall, the furniture was in the same place, in fact, the only thing that was different was the 50-inch flat screen mounted on the wall.

"Daddy didn't change anything," I said, sitting on the black leather couch they bought over four years ago.

"Your daddy wasn't one for decorating," Mommy said, chuckling lightly.

"Kaylen, we've gotta go to the funeral home and take your daddy's suit," she told me.

"We can do that in the morning, I'll call Aunt Yvette and let her know we're here," I replied, pulling out my phone to call daddy's only sister.

"Ok, you do that, and I'll call Reverend James to see if he will officiate," Mommy said.

"Relax ma, we can do all that tomorrow." I said after leaving Aunt Yvette a message letting her know we arrived and were at the house.

"How about Rico and I head out to The Pit to get some food?" I suggested, and everyone agreed.

Stepping out of the house, Rico handed me the keys, and we hopped into his truck. Thirty minutes later, we pulled up to The Pit in downtown Raleigh. They had the best pulled pork and ribs ever. We valeted and headed inside. After placing everyone's orders, we sat at the bar to wait for our food.

"Kaylen, is that you?" I heard a voice say.

I turned around to find Doctor Lynn accompanied by a very nice looking man.

"Hey Doctor Lynn," I said getting up to hug her.

"I didn't know you were in town," she said, hugging me.

"Yea, we got in about an hour ago, my father passed away on Sunday," I told her.

"Oh, Kaylen, I'm so sorry sweetie," she said, hugging me again.

"Thank you," I said, giving her a slight smile.

"The cop that was murdered, that was your father?" She asked, and I nodded.

"When I saw the last name I didn't want to jump to conclusions, but again, I am so sorry, and I hope they catch the bastard that did it," she said.

"So do I," I said.

"Where are my manners? Kaylen, this is my fiancé, Derek," she said, introducing me.

"Nice to meet you, Derek, this is my friend, Rico," I said, making the introductions.

"We've gotta run, but please call me and let me know about the funeral arrangements." Doctor Lynn said, and I agreed as they said goodbye and exited the restaurant.

"That's the doctor you're always talking about?" Rico asked

me, and I nodded. "She seems nice," he said.

"She's helped me through some tough days," I replied, while smiling.

We continued making small talk until our number was called. Rico paid for the food and grabbed the bags. As we were heading out, I noticed Kapri entering.

"Kaylen, oh my goodness, I'm so sorry to hear about your dad," she said, as soon as she spotted me and attempted to hug me.

I gave her a halfhearted hug and looked at the baby she was holding.

"Thanks," I said, with my eyes locked in on the baby.

"Let me know when the funeral is," she said, as her eyes traveled to Rico.

"Hey Rico," she said, smiling.

"Mmmm hmmm," he mumbled, looking annoyed.

"You don't have anything to say to your son?" She asked, lifting the baby boy eye level to Rico.

"Kapri, you and I both know that kid don't belong to me, I left you alone a long time ago." He said, shaking his head while chuckling lightly.

"Yea ok Rico, all I know is you need to take care of your son," she said, rolling her neck.

"Give me a blood test," he challenged.

"Rico, you know damn well he's yours, he looks just like you," she said, angrily.

"Girl, you know that baby don't look nothing like me. You better go holla at his real daddy." Rico said, growing impatient with Kapri's antics.

I took a look at the baby and then glanced at Rico. There were absolutely no similarities between the two; in fact he looked just like...

"Kapri, is that Black's baby?" I asked her with my eyes on the baby, who was the spitting image of Black.

"Huh, what, no, why would you ask me that?" She asked me nervously.

"He looks just like him," I said, looking at her while shaking my head in disgust.

"You tripping Kay, I have never even slept with Black," she said fidgeting, a clear sign that she was lying.

"Rico, let's go," I said, brushing past Kapri.

"I swear Kaylen, he's not Black's baby!" She yelled after me, but I kept walking because if I hadn't, I probably would've slapped the shit out of her.

Doing the math in my head, I realized that she was sleeping with Black while we were together.

"You ok, mama?" Rico asked as we hopped on to I-440.

"Did you know?" I asked him through clenched teeth.

"I mean, I heard stories, but I didn't feed into it because that was your girl, and I didn't think she was on it like that." He said, shrugging.

We rode in silence the whole way back to the house. As we

turned on the block, I saw a bunch of cars lining the street.

"Got damn, the hell all these people come from?" Rico said as we pulled into the driveway behind Aunt Yvette's car.

"My aunt more than likely let them know we were in town, she lives for an audience." I said, feeling a migraine coming. "I'm really not in the mood for this shit," I said, already aggravated, and I hadn't even stepped foot in the house.

"Come on mama, if it gets to be too much, I'll clear everybody out for you," Rico said, causing me to smile at him as we grabbed the bags and got out.

Entering the house, I saw wall-to-wall people, some people I knew, but half of them I'd never even seen before.

"Oh Kaylen, they took my brother," Aunt Yvette screamed as soon as she saw me.

Pulling me into her arms she rocked me back and forth while screaming in my ear, I rolled my eyes slightly at her antics.

Finally, her husband, Tommy, made his way over to us, and carted her off somewhere. I made my way to the kitchen, getting stopped every two seconds by someone offering their condolences. It wasn't that I didn't appreciate it, it was just annoying for people to keep hugging me and saying their sorry every second. We finally reached the kitchen where I found Rae and Sherika hiding out with Aunt Carol.

"Where's Mommy?" I asked them.

"Out back talking to the reverend," Aunt Carol said.

"When did all these people show up?" I asked.

"They showed up right after your extra ass aunt came," Aunt Carol said, rolling her eyes causing us all to laugh.

After a few more minutes, Mommy and Reverend James entered the kitchen. After letting us know that he'd agreed to do the funeral and allow us to use his church, he said his goodbyes and left.

"Carol, can you clear all these people out, I just wanna relax?" Mommy said, rubbing her temples.

"Gladly," she said heading for the living room. "The family appreciates your condolences, but at this time would like a moment to grieve in peace. The funeral and wake arrangements will be posted in tomorrow's paper. They will take visits here at the house for the rest of the week after 5pm, thank you," we heard Aunt Carol say.

"You can't just put these people out, they loved my brother!" I heard Aunt Yvette yell.

Locking eyes with Mommy, I knew this was about to go from bad to worse, so I high tailed it out of the kitchen and into the living room.

"Well, take they ass to your house then, in case you forgot, this is still my sister's house, and they ain't up for all this hoopla," Aunt Carol said just as I entered the living room.

"Who the fu-"

"That's enough! Now, we appreciate all of your love and support, but at this time, my mother and I want to take a moment to finalize arrangements and grieve in peace. You all are more than welcome to stop back by tomorrow," I said, cutting Aunt Yvette off and defusing the situation before it got out of hand while Aunt Yvette grilled Aunt Carol.

People slowly made their way to the door and out of the house. The house was halfway cleared out when I was approached by a tall handsome young man.

"Are you Kaylen?" He asked, looking at me with eyes like Daddy's.

"Yes," I said slowly, looking at him closely.

"I'm SJ, and I'm your brother," he said.

Tears filled my eyes as I looked at SJ, who was definitely Daddy's twin, and pulled him into my embrace. He hugged me tightly as we cried together.

"I'm sorry, it's just that I've been waiting for this moment for years," he said wiping his eyes.

"I never even knew about you." I told him wiping my own tears.

"I knew all about you, Kaylen. Pops was supposed to introduce us a couple years ago, but you had moved out, and I was in college out of state," he explained.

"So, Steve had a son. How old are you, honey?" Aunt Carol asked, scaring me slightly because I forgot she was even in the room.

"I'm twenty-four, ma'am," he said politely.

"What's taking y'all so long the fo-" Mommy said, entering the living room and stopping dead in her tracks. "You're Steve's son," she said, and he nodded.

She rushed to him and pulled him in her embrace.

"I always wondered where you were," she said cradling him.

"Mom, you knew?" I asked in disbelief.

"I've always known Steve had a son before we married, I had just never met him until now," she said grabbing his hand.

"We moved around a lot," SJ said softly, and I could see the pain in his eyes.

I didn't know what he had been through, but from this point on, he was gonna be a permanent fixture in my life.

CHAPTER TWENTY ONE

We spent the next few days getting to know SJ and making the final preparations for Daddy's funeral. I learned that SJ recently graduated from Virginia State University, didn't have any kids and was very smart. He didn't quite go into detail about his childhood, but from the little bit he did share, I could say he'd been through a lot.

His mother, from what I learned, had been on heroin for most of his life. They moved around so much that Daddy couldn't even keep up with him. They reconnected around the same time I moved in with Black.

.I was proud of him because he overcame his obstacles, graduated top of his class and got a full scholarship to Virginia State University where he decided to pursue medicine. He was set to start medical school at Emory University; I was ecstatic that he would be close.

The day of the funeral had finally come, and I was in my old room getting dressed for the funeral when there was a knock on the door.

"Come in," I said, while sliding my feet into my dark blue five inch Giuseppe peep toe pumps.

"You bout ready to go, mama?" Rico asked, entering the room rocking a three piece white Armani suit with a solid blue tie looking rather handsome.

"As ready as I'll ever be," I said, giving myself a once over in the floor length mirror.

We decided that the family would wear dark blue and white since those were Daddy's favorite colors. Sherika helped me find a white Carolina Herrera wrap dress, and I had my hair pulled up into a bun and a simple pair of diamond earrings in my ears.

"I'm right here by your side every step of the way, you know that right?" Rico asked me, looking into my eyes.

"Yes, I know, and I just wanna thank you for being here for us these last few days, it really means a lot," I told him, tearing up.

"I wouldn't have been any place else," he said pulling me into his embrace and kissing the tip of my nose.

We exited the room together and found SJ, Mommy, Aunt Carol, Rae and Sherika sitting in the living room waiting on us.

"You look beautiful, Kay," Mommy said, smiling up at me.

"So do you, Mom," I said, and she did.

Rocking a white Donna Karan pants suit with a silk blue shirt underneath and a pair of four-inch blue Manolo Blahnik pumps, she looked absolutely gorgeous.

"The car is here," Aunt Carol announced, and we all headed out of the house.

I slid into the family car beside Mommy, Aunt Carol and SJ joined us. Rico decided to drive, due to the fact that we had to pick up Aunt Yvette and her husband. Once we picked them up, we headed to St. James Baptist Church. Pulling up to the church, there were cars everywhere, even some police cars were sprinkled in.

"You ready Mommy?" I asked, grabbing her hand.

She took a deep breath and nodded her head as we exited the car. I slid on my dark Chanel bug eyed shades, and Mommy did the same. We lined up in the front of the church with Mommy, SJ and I leading the line. I gripped their hands tightly as the church doors opened, and we proceeded to walk in as everybody stood.

"Would everyone please stand as the family enters the church," Reverend James said.

"There's a place, in heaven, prepared for me, when the tours of this life is over... Where the saints are clothed in white, before the throne, singing praises forever, forever more... In my father's house there are mansions bright, If he said it then I know, I know it's true, yeah yeah... There's a place, for me, beyond, beyond the sky... Brothers and sisters, there's one, ohhhhh, one for you... Jesus he promised, me a home, over

there... Jesus promised, me a home over there... Nooooo more sickness, sorrow, pain and care... Oh, he promised me a home, over there..."

Sister Johnson began to sing Daddy's favorite song, "Jesus Promised Me A Home Over There," beautifully, as we entered the jam packed sanctuary. The closer we got to Daddy's dark blue casket, the tighter I held on to SJ and Mommy. We finally arrived at the casket, and one look at Daddy caused my knees to buckle. Just before I could hit the ground, SJ caught me as I let out a loud wail.

"Daddyyyyyyy!!!!" I screamed before sobbing loudly into SJ's chest.

I was so caught up in my own grief that I didn't notice Mommy lying across Daddy's body, crying her heart out. SJ sat me down in the front pew, and Rico rushed to my side to allow SJ to help Aunt Carol with Mommy.

"Why Lord? Whyyyyyyyy? Stevennnnnnn!!!!!!" Mommy screamed as SJ wrapped his arms around her, pulling her to her seat with tears falling from his own eyes.

We finally got ourselves together somewhat, and the service started. It pretty much went by in a blur for me as I lay my head on Rico's chest and sobbed silently the whole time. Numerous people got up and said good things about Daddy; even the police commissioner got up to say a few words. SJ got up and walked up to the podium.

"Many of you don't know me, but I am Steven Alphonso

Gibson Jr. I have a poem for my dad that I'd like to share," he said, getting choked up.

"Take your time, baby," somebody yelled from the audience.

For a full minute SJ held his head down trying to contain his emotions. Seeing the state that he was in, I got up and stood by his side. Grabbing his hand and giving him a slight smile, I silently encouraged him to read it.

"You never said I'm leaving, you never said goodbye, you were gone before we knew it and only God knows why...

A million times I needed you, a million times I cried, if love alone could've saved you, you would've never died...

In life I loved you dearly, in death I love you still, in my heart I hold a place that only you can fill...

I love you forever, Pops, and I'll carry you with me every day of my life," SJ said, completing his poem with tears in his eyes.

Stepping up to the podium, I cleared my throat before speaking.

"Many of you know me; I'm Kaylen Gibson, Steve's daughter. I just wanna say that my father wasn't perfect by far, but that was my daddy. I know that God doesn't make any mistakes, so I won't question it, but I'm gonna miss my daddy very much," I said, getting choked up as SJ placed his arm around my shoulder. "I just ask that you all keep my family in your prayers as we grieve. Most of you will go back to your respective homes and go on about your day to day life after today. But I ask that you say a small prayer for us and the tough days ahead, thank you," I said, before grabbing my brother's hand and returning to our seats.

Sitting back down next to Rico, he placed a kiss on my cheek and whispered in my ear that I did a good job. After the pastor preached, we had the final viewing. Mom, SJ and I walked hand in hand up to the casket for our final look at Daddy. It didn't feel real at all, Daddy looked like he was just sleeping peacefully in his all white Armani suit and navy blue tie. I leaned down to kiss his cheek and whisper that I love him as SJ did the same. When it was Mommy's turn, she kissed his cold lips as tears fall from her eyes at a rapid pace as we walked her back to her seat where she lay on SJ's shoulder and silently wept.

One by one, people walked up to the casket then over to us to offer condolences. One person in particular made my skin crawl. As I was leaning on Rico's shoulder, I heard a voice I hadn't heard in almost seven months.

"Hey Kay," Black said, standing before me in a three piece black Calvin Klein suit.

I didn't say anything, I just stared at him.

"I'm sorry about your pops, Kay, and I really think we should talk," he said, staring down at my belly.

"I'll call you, because this isn't the time or place," I said staring at him.

"I respect that, Kay," he said nodding his head as he leaned down to kiss my cheek, and out of habit, I jumped slightly, causing Rico to pull me closer while grilling Black.

Nodding his head, Black gave me one last glance before looking at Rico and walking away.

"You good, KK?" Rico whispered in my ear, and I nodded.

The cemetery was one big blur for me. I was all cried out. The only thing left was a void in my heart. We decided not to have a repast, so we headed straight to the house after the burial. Entering my bedroom, I kicked off my shoes and climbed into my bed grabbing the stuffed animal Daddy won for me a few years ago at the state fair and clutched it tightly before drifting off to sleep.

CHAPTER TWENTY TWO

The next few days we spent packing up Daddy's things, deciding on what we wanted to keep and what we wanted to donate to the Goodwill. We had yet to decide whether or not to sell the house or keep it. We had a will reading, and of course, everything was left to Mommy, including a $500,000 life insurance policy. SJ and I each had policies from Daddy, totaling $250,000 each.

Kapri had been by the house every day wanting to talk, but I had nothing to say to her. As far as I was concerned, she didn't exist to me. Mommy had gone to lie down while SJ and I were up talking, when we heard a knock on the door.

"Who is it?" SJ asked, getting up to answer the door.

"It's Black," he said, and SJ turned to look at me.

I gave him a nod, letting him know it was ok, and he opened the door. Black walked in, spoke to SJ, who in turn just stared at him, before sitting down on the couch next to me.

"I'll be in the back, Kay," SJ said while grilling Black.

"So, how you been, Kaylen?" Black asked.

"Happy," I told him honestly.

"I didn't make you happy, Kaylen?" he asked me.

"I'm not going there with you, Cordae, you know the shit you put me through," I said.

"I'm sorry about that shit, ma, a nigga fucked up, but I want you back home, baby," he told me causing me to roll my eyes.

"Your apologies don't mean shit if you just gonna do the same thing again," I said sucking my teeth.

"Is that my baby, Kay?" he asked looking down at my protruding baby bump.

"Unless Jesus Christ himself decided to use me like the Virgin Mary," I replied sarcastically.

"Ain't nobody ask for your smart ass reply," he told me.

"Whatever," I replied rolling me eyes.

"What's up with you and Rico?" he asked me.

"We're just really good friends," I told him while sighing.

"You sure about that, Kay? Because y'all look like more than friends to me," He said.

"Whatever dude, believe what you want," I said, waving him off.

"But since we asking questions, what's up with you and Kapri?" I asked raising an eyebrow.

"What you mean?" he asked looking away guiltily.

"How long have you been fucking her?" I rephrased raising

my voice slightly.

"You tripping, Kay, I ain't never fucked that girl," he said nervously shifting in his seat.

"Then why does her son look like you spit him out," I asked on the verge of losing my cool.

"That ain't my kid, so I don't know," he replied shrugging.

"Get the fuck out, Black! When you're ready to have a honest conversation, then and only then, holla at me," I said getting up from the couch as Black grabbed my wrist tightly causing me to wince in pain.

"The fuck you talking to like that?" He asked through clenched teeth while tightening his grip.

It felt like my wrist was gonna pop at any given time.

"I think she talking to you, my nigga, and I advise you to let her go and get the fuck on like she said," Rico said with venom laced words from behind Black.

"Well look who it is, captain save a hoe," Black said laughing while letting my wrist go and turning around.

Black didn't have a chance to react, as Rico's fist crashed into his jaw dazing him momentarily. Black sent a wild punch toward Rico and missed. Rico hit him with a quick two-piece, dropping Black to his knees. Black rushed Rico and picked him up, slamming him onto his back as the two got it in.

"Stop it, stop it," I screamed to no avail because they kept right on fighting.

SJ pulled me back, and then attempted to break up the fight

only to catch a fist to the jaw from Black. After that, all hell broke loose and it was now two on one.

Mommy came rushing to the front of the house with daddy's shotgun.

BOOM!

She fired a shot into the ceiling, and they immediately stopped fighting.

"Break this shit up right now, before I pull this trigger again," Mommy yelled angrily. "Now clean this mess up, and Black get out of my house! I just buried my husband for Christ sake, and y'all in here acting a damn fool!" she fussed, shaking her head as she headed back to the room.

"I'll see you, my nigga," Black threatened while eyeing Rico.

"I'll be waiting on it, pussy," Rico replied almost too calmly for my liking, with fire dancing in his eyes.

"You too, pretty boy," Rico said to SJ as he headed to the door.

"Don't let the looks fool you, homeboy, this ain't what you want," SJ told him with venom dripping from his tone.

"Before it's all said and done, you'll be back with me, Kay, whether you like it or not," Black said to me before walking out of the door.

"You ok, sis?" SJ asked walking toward me.

"I'm fine, I'm just ready to go home," I said sighing.

"Whenever you're ready, Kay," Rico said pulling me into his arms.

After Black's idiotic performance, we stayed in town for a few more days, packing up Daddy's things and taking them to the Goodwill. We hit the road the following Thursday, I never thought I would be so happy to leave North Carolina in my rear view.

CHAPTER TWENTY THREE

With the money Daddy left me, I purchased a nice three-bedroom townhouse not too far from Sherika in Smyrna, Georgia. Sherika was sad to see me go, but she understood that with the baby coming soon, I needed my own space. Rico and I shopped for my new home, and he helped me arrange everything before he left to go back home.

Now that I was in my own space and Rico was gone, I was super lonely. Mya crossed my mind, so I decided to give her a call.

"Hello," she answered, sounding as if she were whispering.

"Hey Mya, you ok?" I asked, with concern.

"Hey Kay, I'm ok," she replied, still whispering.

"Why are you whispering, Mya?" I asked her.

"It's a long story," she replied while sniffling.

"You know my door is always open, right? You can come here anytime you like," I told to her, and she got really quiet.

"Mya!" I called out to her.

"I gotta go, Kay," she said and hung up before I could respond.

Placing the phone down, I said a silent prayer for Mya before curling up and drifting off to sleep.

"Nooooooo Black, don't," I *screamed.*

"You ain't leaving me this time, Kay," he said sinisterly while raising his gun.

"I won't leave again, I promise," I said with tears in my eyes.

"I know you won't," he said pulling the trigger.

I jumped up in a cold sweat.

I had been having these nightmares for a while now, and I was tired of them. I got up and headed to the baby's nursery to get some things done. I started by washing the baby's clothes, then folded them neatly and placed them in the dresser.

I then neatly stacked the boxes of diapers and baby wipes in the closet. After that was done, I began putting the animal stencils on the wall. Three hours passed, and the nursery was just about done. Rico promised to come and set up the crib when he came back in town.

I headed into the kitchen craving bananas and pickles, with strawberry syrup. After I fixed my snack, I put Jason's Lyric into the DVD player and plopped down on the couch. By the end of the movie, I was in tears, I cried at the ending every time. After the movie was over, I headed to bed because I had an early class tomorrow.

My classes went by pretty quick due to the fact that I only had two. Afterward I decided to hit up the mall and bought the baby some more things. I pulled up to Greenbrier Mall, parked and headed inside. When I exited Baby Gap, I heard someone calling my name; I turned to find Julian jogging toward me.

"Hey Julian," I said smiling at him, genuinely happy to see him.

I hadn't seen Julian since I left NCCU.

"I thought that was you, girl, how you been?" He asked, embracing me.

"I've been good, how about yourself?" I asked him.

"I'm great, now that I see you," he said, winking at me causing me to blush.

"What are you doing in Georgia?" I asked him.

"I decided to do my undergrad at Emory, what are you doing here?" He asked me.

"I live in Smyrna, I've been here since April," I told him.

"We're both in Georgia, only minutes from each other, what are the odds," he said.

"That's crazy right!" I replied, shaking my head.

"I think its fate," he said, looking into my eyes and grabbing my hand.

"What if I don't believe in fate?" I asked him.

"Then I'd say, let me take you to dinner and change your mind," he replied.

"Hmmm, I might be able to do that," I said, smiling at him.

He walked me to my car, and we exchanged numbers, agreeing to meet up later for dinner. Driving home, I could only think of what a coincidence it was that we're both here, I didn't know how ready I was to get in a relationship, but dinner couldn't hurt.

Later that evening Julian took me to Houston's, afterwards we went bowling, and I beat him senselessly, big belly and all. During our third game, Rico called.

"Hey Rico," I answered smiling.

"What's up, mama, what you doing?" He asked me.

"Out bowling with a friend." I told him.

"Bowling? You sure you're supposed to be doing that?" He asked with concern.

"Yes Rico, its fine," I said, shaking my head and smiling.

"Oh ok, just checking. I gotta make sure my little princess is straight," he said.

"My prince is just fine," I replied.

Julian cleared his throat, and looked at me with a look I couldn't quite read.

"Whatever KK, we both know it's a girl," Rico said in my ear.

"Yea Yea Yea, I'll call you when I get home, big head," I told him, as I peeped Julian putting his regular shoes back on.

"Ok mama, love you," Rico said.

"Love you back," I said, and we ended the call.

I placed the phone back into my purse, before turning to an agitated Julian.

"What's your problem?" I asked him with a raised eyebrow.

"I don't have a problem," he replied with attitude.

"It's obvious you do," I said removing my bowling shoes.

"Whatever Kaylen, you ready," he asked standing up.

"You have an attitude for what reason though? I haven't done anything to you," I said in confusion.

"So, talking to another nigga in my face is ok?" He shouted.

"Whoa, first of all, I don't like your tone. Second of all, we are only friends, and third of all, I can talk to whoever I want to," I said, looking at him in disbelief.

"All you females are the same," he mumbled while shaking his head.

"Excuse me? Julian, you are not my man," I said, getting to my feet and grabbing my purse. "I don't know what your problem is, but I have enough on my plate already without the added stress, you have a goodnight," I told, him before walking off.

I was so glad that I decided to drive my own car, because I wanted to get away from Julian as quick as possible.

"Kaylen, wait," Julian called out as I reached my car.

"What Julian?" I asked with attitude as he approached me.

"Listen Kay, I'm sorry, it's just that I really like you, and when I heard you on the phone, I assumed you were talking to your boyfriend," he told me.

"Well, you know what happens when you assume, you make an ass out of yourself. Rico is my best friend and that's it; not that it's any of your business anyway, because you're not my man," I replied, ready to get away from him.

"Please forgive me Kaylen, I truly am sorry, can we start over?" he asked, looking into my eyes.

"I forgive you Julian, but if this happens again, that's it," I told him seriously.

"Thank you, Kaylen, you won't regret it," he said opening my car door, and I slid in.

"Goodnight Kaylen," he said before kissing my cheek.

"Goodnight Julian," I said and pulled off.

You know how Maya Angelou said, "When someone shows you who they are, believe them."

Well, that's what I should've done when Julian had his outburst.

CHAPTER TWENTY FOUR

I was now nine months pregnant and due any day now. School was going great, and I was maintaining a 4.0 GPA. Julian and I had been on several dates, but I wouldn't say we were a couple. We were just having fun with each other. Well, that's how I felt anyway, Julian on the other hand, felt differently, but whatever.

Mommy was coming down, so that someone would be here with me around the clock, and she was staying for a while to help me with the baby. Rico was scheduled to come in town at the end of the week, and I couldn't wait to see him. Julian hated my relationship with Rico, but I explained to him that either he got over it or kicked rocks, because Rico wasn't going anywhere.

Sherika and Rae weren't too fond of Julian; they felt something was off about him. I shrugged it off figuring they were just being overprotective. Black was arrested a month prior for trafficking; he took an eight-year plea deal and was shipped off to a prison in Tennessee. I didn't know how I felt about it, because I still loved Black, but a part of me was relieved.

I was lounging on my couch being lazy when I heard my door open. Since SJ, Rae, Rico and Sherika were the only people with a key, I knew it was one of them.

"Hey fat mama, look who I found," Rae said, kissing my cheek, and Mommy came into view with SJ and Sherika trailing behind.

"SJ, I didn't know you were coming," I squealed excitedly.

"I couldn't miss the birth of my first niece," he said kissing my cheek.

"Don't tell me they brainwashed you into thinking it was a girl," I said rolling my eyes.

"Nope, I just know," he said smiling at me.

"Well hello, Kaylen, or did you not see me come in the door," my mother said sarcastically.

"Sorry Mommy," I said, getting up to hug her.

"Yea Yea Yea," she said, popping my forehead lightly.

"Where's Aunt Carol?" I asked, sitting back down.

"Here I am. I was on the phone with my man honey," Aunt Carol said, grinning from ear to ear.

"Your what!" I shouted.

"My man, child, and he fine too," she said.

"Well go head on then, Auntie," I said, high fiving her.

"What's for dinner?" SJ asked, rubbing his belly.

"Whatever you cook," I smartly replied.

He mushed me, and I popped him on the back of his head.

"Cut it out you two," Mommy scolded us while shaking her head.

"He started it," I said, pouting like a child as everyone laughed.

"Big baby," SJ said, sticking his tongue out.

"Anyway, I'm cooking, what y'all want?" Mommy asked us.

"Smothered pork chops, mashed potatoes, cabbage, macaroni and cheese, cornbread and strawberry cake for dessert," I replied hungrily.

"How you just gon make up the meal for everybody?" Rae asked laughing.

"Everybody? That's for me," I replied seriously, causing everybody to laugh.

"And the sad part about it is, she's serious," Sherika said, shaking her head.

I loved having everybody together at the same time like this; the only person missing was Rico. We were sitting around joking and playing cards, while Mommy cooked dinner with Aunt Carol, when the doorbell rang.

"I'll get it," SJ said going to the door.

"Kaylen, you know somebody named Julian?" SJ shouted from the door.

"Yea, you can let him in," I shouted back.

"Well there goes the neighborhood," Sherika said sarcastically while rolling her eyes.

"Be nice," I told her as SJ came back with Julian in tow.

"Hey everybody," Julian said before kissing my cheek.

"Hey," Sherika and Rae dryly replied.

"The food is ready, guys," Mommy said, entering the room wiping her hands on her apron.

"Ma, this is Julian," I said making the introduction.

"Nice to finally meet you, Mrs. Gibson," Julian said to my mother.

"I would say it's nice to meet you too, but I don't have a clue who you are," Mommy said, bluntly causing Rae and Sherika to giggle.

"I'm Kaylen's boyfriend," he said.

"I wasn't aware that Kaylen had a boyfriend," she said, looking at me with a raised eyebrow.

"Technically, we're just friends," I said, looking at Julian as his jaw clenched.

"Well, it's good to meet you, son, now y'all clean this table off so we can eat. Are you staying for dinner, Julian?" Mommy asked him.

"No ma'am, I was just coming by to check on Kaylen, I have to be going," Julian said.

"Thank God," Rae mumbled, causing Mommy to pop her.

"Enjoy your evening everyone," Julian said, and I walked him outside.

"Did you have to embarrass me like that?" He asked through clenched teeth once we got outside.

"I didn't embarrass you," I told him.

"Then, those two little dyke bitches with their smart ass comments," he said angrily.

"You will not disrespect my family," I told him getting irritated.

"But it's ok for them to disrespect me though right," he said smartly.

"Then you got niggas answering your door and shit," he added.

"That *nigga* is my damn brother! Furthermore, you don't pay the bills here, so you have no say so on who does what in my house," I replied calmly, trying not to lose my cool.

"Why doesn't your mother know about me, huh Kay? I bet you she knows about that nigga, Rico," he shouted angrily.

"It wasn't important for me to tell her about you, we're just **friends!** And of course she knows Rico, you tripping, and I'm not about to stand here in the cold and argue with you. Goodnight Julian," I said before turning to go back in the house.

Julian grabbed my wrist tightly pulling me back to him.

"I don't know who the fuck you think you talking to, but you better show me some got damn respect," he said, glaring at me.

"Julian, I don't know what type of shit you on, but I do know that you need to get your hands off of me right now," I said calmly staring into his eyes.

"Or what?" he asked.

Before I can respond the door opens and out steps SJ, Julian immediately releases his hold.

"You alright Kay?" he asked.

"I'm fine, Julian was just leaving," I said looking at Julian.

"Talk to you later, Kay," Julian said before he climbed into his truck pulling off.

Julian was showing his true colors more and more, but like a fool, I ignored all the warning signs. Besides, I only had those two incidents with Julian, he had been a complete gentleman the times we hung out. He couldn't be like Black, could he?

CHAPTER TWENTY FIVE

November 4th, 2006 at 8:37am, I gave birth to Kadence Ricaí Gibson. Weighing in at 8 pounds 6 ounces, 20 inches long, she had hazel eyes like mine with a nose like Black's. She had a head full of jet-black curly hair and a deep dimple in her left cheek. My baby girl was beautiful. The moment I laid eyes on her, I felt a love I've never felt before.

Rico came to town just in time to see his baby girl (as he calls her) come into the world, he even cut her umbilical cord. Mommy was a ball of water as she and Rico coached me in my delivery. It was bitter sweet because Daddy wasn't here, but I knew he was watching over us from afar.

Everyone was in awe at the new beauty that our family was blessed with. I made Sherika and Rae her godparents; they were ecstatic!

"Aye KK, I think you owe me something, mama," Rico said with Kadence lying on his chest as we all sat around talking.

"What you talking about?" I asked in confusion.

"I won the bet," he said smirking at me, mentioning the bet we made about the sex of the baby.

"Yea Yea Yea, you'll get your money," I said shaking my head.

"Ummmm, Kay, you owe me too remember," Rae said, causing everybody to burst out laughing.

"Me too," SJ and Sherika said in unison.

"You know what, y'all doing the most right now," I said, rolling my eyes.

"Y'all leave my baby alone," Mommy told them.

"Thank you, Mommy," I said, sticking my tongue out at them.

"But quiet as kept, you owe me too," she said.

"Really, Ma?" I asked, looking at her in disbelief.

"I'm just saying," she shrugged as everybody laughed.

"Anyway, Rico, can I hold my baby, please?" I asked him sweetly.

Since she's been back in the room, Rico won't let anybody else hold her, including me!

"She's sleeping, why you wanna mess with her?" He asked me kissing the top of her head.

"Ricooooo," I whined.

"Ok you big baby," he said, getting up and placing her in my arms.

Gazing down at my little angel, I silently thanked God for

142

her. I made a declaration at that moment, to protect her at all cost, and to make sure she never wanted for a thing.

The nurse came in to take the baby to the nursery where she would have her shots and a series of tests done. After Rico asked a million and one questions, she left out with the baby, promising to bring her back in a couple of hours.

"I'm hungry," Rae said.

"Me too," I agreed.

"Yo ass always hungry," SJ said jokingly.

"I know you grown, but you better watch that mouth, Steven Jr," Mommy said sternly.

"Sorry ma" he replied sheepishly.

"Anyway, what we eating?" I asked.

"I want some wings from Hooters," Sherika said and everybody agreed.

After placing our order, Rae, Sherika and SJ headed out.

"I'm going to go call your Aunt Yvette and let her know you had the baby," Mommy said, leaving out the room.

Rico and I chatted for a little while before the exhaustion of the delivery, mixed with the meds took me into a deep slumber. I didn't know how long I was out, but when I woke up it was dark out. Looking to my left, I saw Rico stretched out on the pullout bed with Kadence lying on his chest.

For a moment, I just watched the two of them sleep. I truly thanked God for placing Rico in my life when he did. Without him, I honestly don't know where I would be right now. I got out of the bed slowly and headed to the bathroom.

After brushing my teeth and washing up, I took off the hospital gown and put on the pajama set Mommy brought me. I pulled my long mane into a ponytail, and walked back into the room as Kadence started to whine. Walking over to Rico, I tried to gently remove her from his grasp.

"What you doing?" he asked me, waking up.

"It's time for her to eat," I told him, cradling her into my arms and sitting back on the bed.

I pull out my breast, and she latched on hungrily as I nursed her.

"I wanna sign her birth certificate," Rico said out the blue.

"You don't have to do that, Rico," I told him watching Kadence feed off of my breast.

"I know I don't have to, but I want to," he said seriously causing me to look up at him.

"I may not be her father biologically, but that's my lil mama right there, and it ain't a muthafucka in this world that could tell me any different," he said, causing my eyes to water.

"I appreciate everything you've done for me, Rico, and I would be honored for you to sign her birth certificate," I told him as the tears fell down my face.

Rico approached me slowly, and then planted a soft kiss on my lips.

"I love you, Kaylen," he told me looking into my eyes.

"I love you, too, Rico," I replied, smiling at him.

For the rest of the night, we talked and made plans for Kadence's future. I'm torn on whether or not to send Black pictures. I mean, technically she is his daughter, but I don't know how I feel about him having a relationship with her.

I was released from the hospital two days later. The gang got together and threw me a welcome home party with two special guests.

"Myaaaaaa!" I screamed rushing into her arms.

"Gosh, I missed you so much, Kay," she said, embracing me.

"I missed you, too, girl," I told her.

"I know that's not my baby," I said looking at the handsome little man hiding behind her legs,

"AJ, come say hi," she said, pulling him from behind her.

"He's so big," I said, as I kneeled down to hug him.

"Well, I hope you're happy to see me too," a voice said from behind me.

I turned around and came face to face with Doctor Lynn. I rushed into her arms I gave her a big hug.

"It's so good to see you, now where is that baby?" she asked, smiling at me.

"I'm willing to bet Rico is somewhere hogging her from everybody," I told her, and my assumption was correct.

They fawned all over the baby and also gave me an impromptu baby shower. Kadence had so much stuff; I wouldn't have to buy anything for the next two years.

All was going well in our lives, but nothing too good lasts

forever. The next few years, literally almost broke me down to my knees!

CHAPTER TWENTY SIX

I thought about taking the spring semester off so I could focus on raising Kadence, but Rico and Mommy weren't having it, so Mommy stayed with me to help out with the baby so I could return to school.   Rico decided to head back home when Kadence turned two months, and I was sad to see him go, but I understood.

"Kaylen, bring me a sleeper for Tootie," Mommy yelled from the bathroom.

Tootie was the nickname mommy gave Kadence. Where it came from, I couldn't tell you.

"Here you go, Ma," I said, entering the bathroom.

Hearing the sound of my voice, Kadence turned her head toward me, giving me a smile full of gums.

"Hey pretty girl," I cooed, causing her to kick her feet happily, splashing water.

Kadence was now five months old, and fat as a butterball.

She was such a happy baby always smiling and hardly ever crying.

Julian and I had decided to slowly enter into a relationship; to say everybody was pissed would be an understatement. Nobody was more upset than Rico. He hated Julian with a passion, but what could he do about it? I was a grown ass woman, and Julian made me happy. I decided to keep Black updated on Kadence's progress, even though we ended in a bad place, she was still his daughter.

He sent me a letter sincerely apologizing for all the bullshit he put me through; I remember it clear as day.

Kaylen,

First, I wanna say thank you for giving me a beautiful baby girl and allowing me in to her life, even if only through pictures. Also, I wanna apologize from the bottom of my heart for the shit I put you through. I didn't realize how wrong it was until I saw the pictures of Kadence; knowing I would kill a nigga for doing half of the shit I did to you to her. Growing up I watched my father beat on my mother, and I saw my grandfather do the same to my grandmother, I thought that was what love was all about, so I abused women too. I know that's not an excuse, and I now realize that I'm no better than them. I do love you Kaylen and I always will, but I know that we can never be together again and I'm finally at peace with that. I just want you to be happy Kay, because your happiness affects Kadence's happiness. I just hope that you can find it in your heart to forgive me. I need your forgiveness Kay. Once again I thank you for giving me a beautiful baby girl and for the pictures you sent to me. I love you Kaylen, never forget that!

Love Always,
Cordae

After receiving Black's letter I went to visit him, and we had a very long talk about everything, he even gave me his blessing to move on. The time he was doing was really having a good impact on him, and I could honestly say that I felt free. I knew that I had to forgive Black, not for him, but in order for me to move on with my life, so I did.

"What time you leaving, Kay?" Mommy asked me walking into the kitchen cradling Kadence.

"Julian should be here any minute," I told her.

"You guys getting pretty close huh?" She asked as she began to feed the baby.

"You can say that," I replied.

"Well, as long as he makes you happy, baby," she said softly.

"What do you think about him mama, honestly," I asked her.

"He's ok," she said.

"Just ok?" I asked with a raised eyebrow.

"What do you want me to say, Kay, I don't care for him too much, but that's your business. You're the one that gotta be with him, not me, so it shouldn't matter how I feel," she replied.

Before I could respond the doorbell rung, and I went to answer it.

"Hey gorgeous," Julian said as I opened the door.

"Hey Julian," I said, embracing him as he entered the house.

"You ready to go?" he asked.

"Yea, just let me grab my purse and jacket," I said as Mommy exited the kitchen.

"Hello Mrs. Gibson," he said politely.

"Hey Julian," she replied.

"Hi little Miss Kadence," he cooed, and she looked at him strangely.

For some reason, she didn't take to Julian very well. Every time he picked her up, she screamed. Sherika said it was because Julian was the devil, and babies are sensitive to people's energies. I say, it's because Rico and SJ had her so spoiled, she didn't want any parts of another man, every time she sees one of them she lights up.

"I'm gone mama, I'll be back later," I said before kissing her and Kadence, then heading out with Julian.

We enjoyed a nice dinner at Murphy's, a nice American restaurant in Marietta. We then decided to do some dancing at Sutra Lounge, a nice chic lounge on Crescent Ave. The atmosphere was nice and laid back, as we enjoyed each other's company and danced the night away. On the way back to my house, we talked about our relationship and the future.

"I want you guys to move in with me," Julian said.

"I don't know, Julian, that's such a big step," I replied a little hesitant.

"Just think about it, it'll be good for Kadence to have a father figure around every day," he said.

"Kadence has a father Julian, in fact she has two that love her very much," I said becoming agitated.

"One is in prison, the other is here today, gone tomorrow, be serious, Kaylen," he replied smugly.

"I'm not in the mood for this conversation right now, this is why I don't think it's a good idea for us to move in together," I said, rubbing my temples.

I felt an instant headache coming.

"I'm sorry Kaylen, I just want what's best for you and Kadence," he replied, grabbing my hand into his.

"And I appreciate that, but right now I don't think us moving in together is a good idea. We just got together, and our relationship is still very new," I explained to him.

"Just take it into consideration, ok," he said, and I nodded as we pulled up to my house.

I kissed him softly before hopping out of the truck and going inside the house. Was I really ready to live with another man?

CHAPTER TWENTY SEVEN

Things had been going well, and I was about to enter my junior year of college. Kadence was eight months old and started to look like Black more every day. She was growing up so fast and was crawling around getting into everything! Julian and I were doing great as well; in fact I decided to move in with him.

I kept my own place though, just as a precaution, if it didn't work out too well. Mommy wanted to protest, but decided against it, and headed back to Augusta with Aunt Carol. Sherika and Rae flat out refused to come visit me once I moved in with Julian, so if I wanted to see them, I had to go to their place.

We were having an engagement party for Sherika and Rae at their place. I arrived early to help them set up for the party.

"Kaylen, you talked to Rico lately?" Sherika asked me.

"Yea, I talked to him the other day, he should be here any minute now," I said arranging the food on the table.

"Before he gets here, you should know tha-"

The doorbell interrupted our conversation. I picked Kadence up off the floor and headed to the door. Opening the door I come face to face with Rico, who Kadence immediately reaches for, next to him is a female I've never seen before.

"Hey baby girl," Rico cooed tickling Kadence causing her to giggle.

"Hey Kay, I want you to meet my girlfriend, Iyana," he said introducing us.

Did he just say his girlfriend? I instantly feel a pain in my chest. I never thought about Rico ever dating anyone, but to see him with her, made me feel sick to my stomach.

"Nice to meet you, Iyana," I said, through a forced smile.

"I've heard a lot about you, Kaylen," she said smiling sweetly.

Iyana was very pretty, she was about 5'5", brown skin, slanted brown eyes, rocking a short spiked haircut and has a very nice shape.

"And you must be Kadence," she said grabbing her hand.

Kadence looked at her strangely, snatched her hand back and then looked at Rico. I couldn't help the smirk that crossed my face.

"Your sister is in the kitchen, I need to go change Tootie," I said, grabbing her and heading upstairs.

Once I entered the bedroom, my heart broke and tears come to my eyes. I know it might have been selfish, but I didn't want Rico to be with anybody else, he was supposed to wait for me. I know I sounded like a complete hypocrite because I was with Julian, but I didn't care. After I changed Kadence, I headed back downstairs and saw that Mommy, SJ and Aunt Carol had arrived.

"There goes my little toot toot," Mommy squealed grabbing her out of my arms and planting kisses all over her face.

SJ and Aunt Carol did the same completely ignoring my presence.

"Well, I'm doing fine thanks for asking," I said sarcastically.

"Hey Kay," Mommy said, not even looking at me.

"Hey sis," SJ said, kissing my cheek.

"Yea Yea Yea," I said as I mushed him.

"Come here, let me holla at you for a minute," Aunt Carol said then pulled me into the foyer.

"What's up Auntie?" I asked her.

"You know Rico is here with some female, don't you?" she asked me.

"Yes Auntie, and I'm happy for him," I replied, lying through my teeth.

"Yea ok, and I'm boo boo the fool," she said sarcastically.

"Really auntie, I am. It's not like we were together or anything. Besides I'm with Julian now," I reminded her.

"You may be with Julian, but your heart is with Rico. I know it's tearing you up inside to see him with that girl, but he wasn't gon wait forever, Kay. Hell, I thought you would've been done came to your senses and gave him a chance. Especially after the way he stepped up, and decided to raise Tootie as if she were his

155

own. But things happen the way they're supposed to, I guess. Anyway, let's get back to this party before they come searching for us," Aunt Carol said before walking off leaving me deep in thought.

I stood in the same spot for a good ten minutes, before joining the rest of the gang in the living room. It pained me to see Rico smiling and laughing with Iyana. Julian wasn't invited, so I was here alone. The whole scene literally started to make me sick, so I decided to leave early.

"You leaving already, Kay?" Rae asked me as I gathered our things.

"Yea, I'm not feeling too well," I told her.

"You can go upstairs and lay down if you want," she offered.

"No thanks, I really just wanna go home and get some rest," I said, putting on my coat and grabbing the baby's.

"Well, we can keep Tootie tonight so you can get some rest" she told me.

"You don't have to do that," I said.

"Girl, it's no trouble, and besides she's our God daughter. Plus, she has everything she needs here," she said, and I agreed to let her stay.

"I'll call you guys later," I told her as I headed to the door.

"Ok and get some rest, Kay," she said, and I nodded before walking out the door, not saying goodbye to anybody.

I was with Julian, so why was Rico's new relationship breaking my heart? I wanted to be with Julian, or so I thought.

Seeing him with Iyana finally confirmed what I had been trying to deny, I was definitely in love with Rico.

CHAPTER TWENTY EIGHT

I remember the first time Julian hit me very well. We had been living together for about six months at that point; Rico had called one day to inform me that he deposited money into my account.

Rico didn't want me to work while I was in school and the fact that I had Kadence now, it was too much for me to try and work. Once a month, Rico deposited $5,000 into my account, for "child support", as he called it. I tried to protest after I'd gotten Daddy's insurance check, but he told me to put that in the bank and save it for a rainy day.

Julian wasn't too pleased at the fact that Rico took care of me and Kadence. We got into a big blow up about it, I remember it well...

"You fucking this nigga or something, Kaylen? I mean, I don't know no nigga that do shit like that for free," he yelled.

"Are you serious right now? You knew the deal with me and

Rico before you came into the picture! He's my best friend, and he isn't going anywhere, either deal with it or leave," I yelled back frustrated.

I was so happy that Tootie was with Mommy for the week.

"What kind of man would I be if I let another nigga take care of my woman and daughter?" he asked me.

"SHE'S NOT YOUR DAUGHTER!" I screamed, becoming frustrated with the whole conversation.

"She ain't Rico daughter either," he said smugly.

"He's more of her father then you'll ever be," I mumbled, but apparently not low enough.

SMACK!

Julian landed a vicious backhand to my face, splitting my lip instantly.

"You gone learn to fucking respect me, Kaylen!" he screamed, grabbing me by my hair and slamming me into the wall.

Panic and fear consumed me. Julian looked at me evilly, almost looking like Lucifer himself.

"Look what you made me do, Kay, I never wanted you to see this side of me," he said pacing back and forth in front of, me rubbing his hands over his head.

"I'm sorry," I softly whispered holding my aching head.

"You not sorry yet, but you will be," he said walking toward me.

That night Julian beat me with his belt; over and over again he hit me, careful not to bruise my arms, legs and face. After he finished beating me, he locked me in the hall closet, where I stayed for three days. I didn't eat the whole three days I was locked in there; hell, he barely gave me water.

I was so weak by the time he let me out of there, but when he did, he was a totally different person. He ran me a hot bath, fed me and massaged my body.

"You know, Kaylen; I didn't wanna have to do that to you. But I need for you to understand that I'm a man with feelings, and I don't appreciate you running to Rico every time you or Kadence need something. I'm your man honey, let me be all you need," he said as he washed my weak body.

I didn't even respond, I just silently wept as I stared off into space.

Why is this my life? Am I just destined to go through hell all my life? Here I was, not even twenty-one yet, and I was on my second abusive relationship. I thought about leaving, but maybe Julian was right, if I allowed him to take care of me and stop accepting money from Rico, then we would be ok. I mean, what man wants to compete with another man?

I even thought about calling SJ or Rico and telling them what he did to me. But it only happened this one time; surely it wouldn't happen again, would it?

Besides, I needed to handle my life on my own and stop running to Rico whenever things got hard. So yes, I kept my mouth shut about everything and even when I went to pick up

Tootie from my mother, I put a phony smile on my face.

What I didn't know at the time was that I was exposing my daughter to the same things my mother exposed me to. It's funny how history has a way of repeating itself, or how we as people succumb to generational curses.

I had left one horrible relationship for an even worse one. Inside I felt like this was my fate, I mean, why else would I get with the same type of man as Black, or hell even my father for that matter. What was it about me that kept attracting these types of men?

I was too ashamed to admit that I was in the same type of situation as before, so I stayed away from everybody. I was beat down so much mentally and emotionally that I didn't know what to do anymore.

I felt like God was punishing me for some reason, so I stopped praying. Eventually I stopped going to school, I was TIRED of living this life.

I loved my daughter more than life itself, but how could I be the best mother to her right now? I wasn't sure, so I asked Mommy to keep her for a few months while I got myself together, it was one of the hardest things I've ever had to do. But I couldn't risk her getting hurt if Julian decided one day to unleash his wrath upon her.

One thing was for certain though, something had to give because I wasn't 100% sure that I could make it through this one.

CHAPTER TWENTY NINE

Once Kadence was gone the abuse got even worse. Julian was like Dr. Jekyll and Mr. Hyde, one minute he was sweet and understanding. Then in an instant, he'd flip and whoop my ass if I said the wrong thing.

One day I was in the kitchen cooking dinner. He stormed into the house and punched me so hard in my back that I thought he had broken something. Or another time when Jazzie had mistakenly chewed one of his Louboutin sneakers, he punched me in my face instantly blacking my left eye.

I never saw Jazzie again after that. I was hurt; Jazzie was like family, now she was gone. I didn't know what to do anymore. I had isolated myself from my family and friends.

Rico, Sherika and Rae called everyday nonstop, but I never answered, I hadn't talked to them in about five months. In fact, the only person I ever answered for was Mommy, and that was because she had my daughter. She often asked what was going on with me, I would always lie and said school was keeping me busy. I was slowly accepting my fate; I had become numb to everything.

"Kaylen, bring your ass in here," Julian yelled from the living room, and I hurriedly made my way to him.

"We're having dinner with my parents tonight, dress nice and don't embarrass me," he said, glaring at me.

I didn't even say anything; I simply nodded and headed upstairs. I HATED Julian's parents; they were so stuck up and phony as hell. His mother was the biggest bitch I'd ever met, she constantly ranted about Julian being with me.

She felt as though I wasn't from the right "breed", whatever the hell that meant. I stood in the closet looking around at all this materialistic bullshit. I would give it all back in a heartbeat if it meant getting out of this hellhole.

Finally, I selected a simple black Donna Karan wrap dress that accentuated my curves; I paired it with a pair of gold Giuseppe ankle booties. I quickly showered and got dressed, then headed down to meet Julian.

"Wow, you look gorgeous," he complimented me causing me to damn near break my neck to look at him.

This was the first time Julian had complimented me in a long time.

"Thank you," I softly replied.

He grabbed my hand, locked up the house and helped me into the truck. We then headed to Buckhead to have dinner with the

Huxtables.   We pulled up to their sprawling mansion approximately forty minutes later. Julian helped me out of the truck, and we headed to the door.

"Hello, Master Julian, Miss Kaylen," the butler, Carl, said.

"Hey Carl," Julian replied, and I followed suit.

After taking our jackets, we headed into the sitting area where we found Julian's parents, Paulette and David, along with his siblings and their significant others.   Julian had two older brothers, David Jr. who is an egotistical ass hole, with a plastic ass wife named Rebecca.   Johnathan and his wife Adriana, who were both cool as hell, the only ones I genuinely liked out of the Green clan.

"Hello Mother," Julian said kissing her cheek.

"Hey honey," she said and then laid eyes on me.

"Kaylen," she said dryly.

"Paulette," I replied even drier.

"Hello Kaylen, how are you?" David Sr asked me pleasantly.

"I'm fine sir, how about you?" I asked politely.

"I can't complain," he replied pleasantly.

"Hey Kay," Johnathan said smiling.

"Hey Johnathan," I said smiling back.

Adriana got up and embraced me tightly.

"I'm so glad you're here, I thought I was gonna have to slap the shit out of one of these bitches," she whispered, and I stifled a laugh.

Paulette hated Adriana almost as much as she hated me, I'm

assuming it's because we didn't kiss her ass like Rebecca did.

Johnathan was kind of an outcast himself. Instead of going to Yale or Harvard like they wanted him to, he decided to go to Morehouse and major in sports medicine instead of law. David Jr., on the other hand, went to Harvard Law School where he met Rebecca. They're both egotistical jackasses.

Adriana was a social worker and had a master's degree from Clark Atlanta. She was a beautiful Spanish chica from Brooklyn, standing at 5'4 smooth caramel skin, slanted gray eyes, long wavy hair and a body that wouldn't quit. I thought her and Jonathan complimented each other very well.

Rebecca was just, plain. Standing at 5'8, pale as hell, icy blue eyes with huge breasts and no ass whatsoever, but you couldn't tell that bitch she wasn't cute.

As expected, neither one of them spoke. I didn't bother to speak either. They could both kiss my round ass.

"Julian dear, I ran into Samantha the other day, she just graduated top of her class at Yale Law. She misses you, and I know you miss her too, so I invited her over for dinner," Paulette said, smirking at me.

I wanted to shout, "I DON'T GIVE A DAMN!" Hell, she could have him by all means; I wouldn't even put up a fight! Before Julian could respond the doorbell rang and moments later this toothpick of a girl walked into the room.

"Samantha, I'm so glad you made it," Paulette said as she embraced her, and I locked eyes with Adriana.

Samantha is cute, but that's about it. She's about 5'7 tanned skin, green eyes, long auburn hair and no curves anywhere.

"Hello Julian," she said, embracing him, and he embraced her back, a little too long for someone who had a girlfriend if you asked me.

"Wow, it's been awhile, how you been?" he asked smiling at her, as if I wasn't sitting here.

"I'm great now. I've been thinking about you a lot lately, and I hated how things ended between us," she said pouting her botox filled lips.

Adriana gave me a 'what the fuck' look, and I simply shrugged. I couldn't care less about the blatant disrespect from these two. Hell if I had my way, I would hand Julian over to her ass gladly!

"You two look so good together," Paulette said then grinned at me.

I wanted so badly to give her my finger, but I kept my composure and gave her a smug look.

"Samantha, this is my girlfriend, Kaylen, Kaylen meet Samantha," Julian said, finally acknowledging my presence.

"Nice to meet you, Karen," Samantha said, smugly, intentionally mispronouncing my name.

"It's Kaylen, actually," I said, smirking at her.

"Sorry, you say tomatoes, I say tomato," she shrugged and turned to Julian completely dismissing me.

"Anyway, Julian we must get together soon, I mean, if it's ok with Kayla," she said, looking at me with the fakest smile plastered on her face.

"Her name is Kaylen, damn!" Adriana said with irritation.

"Adriana, how nice to see you, you and Johnathan still together huh? Who would've thought?" she asked, nastily.

I saw Adriana's eyes turn into slits, and I already knew she was about to pop off.

"Listen putā, I am not the one, so if you know what's good for you, you'll fall back before you find yourself with a whooped ass!" Adriana said calmly, her accent thick, which often happened when she was pissed.

"Johnathan, do you see what type of filth you have allowed into your life? I swear I don't see where we went wrong with you," Paulette said disgustingly, pouring kerosene on top of an already burning fire.

"You are my mother and I love you, but you will not disrespect my wife, and until you can show her some respect, I will not step foot back into this house!" Johnathan said, grabbing a fired up Adriana and storming out.

"Well, that's just great because she's not welcomed back into my house! While you're at it, take Julian's whore with you," Paulette spat venomously looking in my direction.

"I didn't want to come here anyway, so I have no problem with leaving, to hell with you Paulette. You love insulting people only to make yourself look good, but you're only making yourself look like an ignorant bitch! If you were on fire, I wouldn't even spit on you, who the hell are you to judge anybody? Instead of hating you, I actually feel sorry for you because you think your life is so squeaky clean and you're on some type of pedestal, but in reality it isn't as clean as you think it is, isn't that right, Mr. Green?" I spat and smirked, while getting up and followed them out the door, leaving everybody in the room with their mouths wide open.

I knew I would have hell to pay when Julian came home, but at the moment I didn't give a damn! I was sick of everything at this point, fuck it; my life couldn't get any worse, could it?

CHAPTER THIRTY

Julian got home around 3am. I know because he woke me up snatching me out of bed by my hair so tightly I thought he was going to rip it from my head. That night he beat my ass something terrible, and for the first time I actually fought back, which only made him angrier.

"Oh, so you wanna get tough and fight me back you little bitch? I got something for your ass!" he screamed grabbing me by throat as he ripped my pajamas from my body.

He threw me on the bed and pressed my face into a pillow, please don't let him do what I think he's about to do, I silently pray as tears fill my eyes.

Now, either God didn't like me, or he was on vacation or something, because the next thing I knew Julian grabbed his thick eight-inch dick, spit on it and rammed it into my virgin ass hole.

"Ahhhhhhhhhh!" I screamed into the pillow as tears rolled

down my face.

I was trying to pull away but couldn't because he held me in place. The pain was unbearable, it felt like my ass was being ripped apart and somebody poured alcohol on it.

"I'll show you to respect me, you little ungrateful bitch," Julian yelled then moaned as he pumped in and out of me.

I was in complete shock as he continued to violate me, over and over again. I was being raped yet again by someone that claimed to love me. It was at that moment that I began to hate God; it was obvious that he didn't give a damn about me, or He wouldn't have allowed this to keep happening to me.

By the time Julian was finished, I was in a daze, I ached all over, and the sheets were covered in blood.

Julian just looked at me smugly and said, "Go get yourself cleaned up, and you better not get blood on my fucking carpet!"

My whole body was on fire as I limped to the bathroom, and I just wanted it all to be over. I ran me a hot bath and locked the bathroom door, before searching the medicine cabinet and finding my bottle of Vicodin. Popping open the bottle of Vicodin, I swallowed one pill, then another, then another and another until the whole bottle was gone. Then I eased inside the tub and allowed the pills to take me far away from this hellhole.

I felt my heart beat quicken and my body went numb, I smiled slightly knowing that it wouldn't be long now, a few minutes later everything went black.

"Baby girl," I heard a voice said, and I turned to see my

daddy walking towards me.

"Daddy," I screamed rushing into his arms.

"You shouldn't be here baby girl," he said, hugging me tightly.

"I'd rather be here Daddy, life is just too hard," I said with tears in my eyes.

"You can't give up baby girl, not now, you have a child that needs you. God is not done with you yet. It's time for you to fight, Kaylen! I know that the things you saw me and your mother go through have had an impact on the type of relationships you have had. What I did to your mother was wrong, and it took her leaving me to finally see the error of my ways. When she left me I was destroyed and didn't want to live anymore. I ended up on the church steps one Sunday and no matter how many times I tried to leave, I couldn't. That day I made the decision to surrender myself to the Lord, I had been going there for a while when I reached out to your mother. As expected, she didn't have anything to say to me, then I ended up here. My work on earth was done, I love you baby girl, but right now it's not your time," he said looking me in the eyes.

"God doesn't care about me, Daddy, if he did he wouldn't allow me to keep going through this!" I shouted angrily.

"Don't you ever say that again, God loves you very much, Kaylen, and He would never put more on you than you can bear!" he said sternly.

"This is too much for me to bear, Daddy, I'm tired of it all,

there is no more fight in me!" I said, feeling defeated.

"Nonsense, you're a Gibson, and we don't give up, we fight! You have someone else to fight for now. It's not your time, Kaylen, and you still have work to do," he said grabbing my shoulders tightly.

"But Daddy, I don't wanna leave, I wanna stay with you," I started to cry uncontrollably.

"I'll always be with you, baby girl, as long as you keep me in your heart, I'll never be far away. I want you to get yourself together, if not for yourself do it for that precious baby girl you have. You've always been a fighter, Kaylen, you can't give up now baby girl," he said.

"I don't wanna fight, Daddy, I'm tired," I told him weakly.

"You gotta fight, Kaylen, you have to! Now I gotta get going, but you remember what I said and know that I love you very much, baby girl. Let your mother and brother know that I love them, and kiss that beautiful baby for me," he said before kissing my forehead and turning to walk away.

"Daddyyyyyyy!" I screamed after him, but he kept walking.

"Fight Kaylen," he said and then he disappeared as I fell to my knees crying.

"CLEAR!" I heard somebody yell and then my body convulsed.

"We got her back," I heard somebody else scream.

All of a sudden I felt an object being forced down my throat, and I gagged instantly, before I felt the inside of my stomach being emptied.

"That's right darling, throw it all up," I heard a gentle voice say as I continued to vomit up everything in my stomach.

What's happening? Where's my daddy? Where am I? My mind screamed question after question as I continued to feel my stomach being emptied.

I felt a warm hand rubbing my hair softly. Why can't I move? Why can't I open my eyes? I start to panic and I heard a machine begin beeping like crazy.

"She's crashing again!" I heard somebody yell and then I didn't hear anything as everything went black.

What feels like years later, I opened my eyes and the brightness of the light caused me to close them back. I slowly opened them again and allowed my eyes to adjust. I took a look around and realized I was in a hospital room.

Looking to my left, I saw Rae, SJ and Sherika curled up together on the small couch asleep. The sight was surely a hilarious one, and I probably could've laughed if it wasn't for the tube in my throat. Looking to my right, I saw Rico stretched out in an uncomfortable looking chair and my heart cried. These people loved me so much that they were all camped out in this room for me, and I foolishly turned them away. Tears fell down my face, and I reached up to wipe them away, only to notice restraints on my wrists, the rattling of the bed rail caused Rico to spring up out of his seat.

"KK, you're awake!" Rico said, loudly waking the others as

they rushed to my side.

Rico pressed the button for the nurse, and a few minutes later she entered the room followed by a doctor.

"Welcome back Miss Gibson, I'm Doctor Neal," he said removing the restraints.

I rubbed my sore wrists as they checked my vitals and removed the tube from my throat. Once the tube was out, I tried to speak and it came out hoarsely.

"I'll get you some ice water," the nurse said rushing out of the room and returning moments later with a bottle of Aquafina and a cup of ice.

She filled the cup with water and put the straw to my mouth; the cold water instantly soothed my sore throat as I drank until it was completely gone.

"How are you feeling, Miss Gibson?" Doctor Neal asked.

"Like I got hit by a dump truck, how long have I been here," I asked in as raspy tone.

"You've been here for almost two weeks," he said, and my eyes bulged.

"Wow, I've been out that long?" I asked in disbelief.

"You gave us quite a scare in the beginning, you flat lined twice and then we had to give you a sedative to calm you down. You were pretty banged up when you got here, can you tell us what happened?" he asked.

"I don't remember. How did I get here?" I asked curiously.

"That we don't know, one of the nurses came out on her break and saw you lying in front of the ER doors in a bathrobe. We didn't know how long you'd been there, but you were unresponsive," Doctor Neal told me.

Wow, how cruel can someone be? If Julian was just gonna discard me like trash, he should've left me alone to die. At that moment, I realized that Julian didn't give a damn about me, and my hate for him multiplied times one hundred!

"Well, your wounds have healed nicely, and we'd like to keep you here for a few more days for observation. I'd also like for you to go down and talk to our hospital psychiatrist," he said.

"I'm not crazy, Doc," I said, and he chuckled lightly.

"Well, it's standard procedure for all suicide patients, but I'll make an exception for you, as long as you promise to go talk to someone," he said, looking at me sternly.

"She will, Doc. I'll make sure of it," Rico said, speaking for me.

"So will we," the double mint twins replied.

"Me too," SJ said looking at me with tears in his eyes causing my own to fill.

At that moment, I realized just how much my actions had affected everyone around me.

"Very well, I'll release you in a few days," he said and left the room.

"Don't you ever scare us like that ever again!" Sherika cried, hugging me tightly.

"I'm sorry guys, I just didn't wanna live anymore," I told them softly, as tears fell from my eyes.

"What happened, mama?" Rico asked, sitting next to me.

"I don't wanna talk about it," I said, putting my head down.

"Did that punk ass nigga do this to you?" Rae asked, and I dropped my head.

"Ah hell nah, I'm gon fuck that nigga up!" SJ screamed and headed for the door.

"SJ, just let it go," I cried out.

"Nah sis, he almost took you away from us! Is that the reason you've been so distant?" he asked angrily, as tears fell rapidly from his eyes.

"It was so much going on. I had gotten myself into another bad situation, and I didn't wanna burden any of you with my problems. You all were so happy in your lives, and I didn't want my drama to complicate things, so I stayed away," I said, honestly as the tears fell down my face.

"Kaylen, you know that no matter what you got going on, we're always here for you, me in particular," Rico said, embracing me as I laid my head on his chest.

"We're all here for you, Kay, I knew something was up, I just couldn't put my finger on it," Sherika said, wiping her tears.

"You know we gotta call mama and let her know you're up, she's been a mess since we found out," Rae said, and I cried harder, just knowing how much pain I caused them.

"How is my baby?" I asked Rico through tear filled eyes.

"She's good, but she missed her mommy," Rico said.

I almost left my child without a mother, what the hell was I thinking? The floodgates opened at the thought, and I sobbed uncontrollably as Rico hugged me tighter.

"I'm so sorry," I apologized over and over again softly as I sobbed into Rico's chest.

"It's ok mama, the only thing that matters is that you're still here," Rico said, kissing my forehead.

"I want to see my baby," I said, looking up at Rico.

"I texted Ma while you were talking, they're on the way," Sherika told me.

We sat around talking and catching up. For the first time in what seemed like months, I actually laughed. Thirty minutes later, Mommy rushed in followed by Aunt Carol and an 18-month-old walking Kadence.

"Praise the Lord my baby is alright, thank you Jesus," Mommy said with tears in her eyes as she hugged me tightly.

"Girl, if you ever scare us like that again I will whoop your ass, you hear me," Aunt Carol said with tears in her eyes as she hugged me, and I nodded.

"Da-Da up up," Kadence said as Rico picked her up and she immediately reached for me.

"Hey mama's baby, I'm so sorry," I said, through my tears as I grabbed her in my arms and hugged her tightly.

"I love you so much," I said, kissing all over her chubby little cheeks.

"Ma ma," she said giving me a slobber filled kiss, and it was the best kiss I'd ever had.

I looked around the room at the people that I loved more than anything in the whole world, and I made a declaration to get it together, not only for them but most importantly for myself and Kadence. God was keeping me alive for some reason, and I was going to fight, just like my daddy told me to.

CHAPTER THIRTY ONE

The first step to getting myself together was cuttting off all communication with Julian. While he was at work one day, we went and removed all my things from his house. I didn't want anything except Kadence's baby book and my pictures. Everything Julian bought me was taken to the goodwill.

Rico thought it was a good idea to sell my townhouse, and find another place since Julian knew where I lived. I didn't go to Sherika and Rae's either because he'd look for me there, so SJ told me I could to stay with him for as long as I wanted.

I ended up getting my number changed because Julian called and texted nonstop. I even left Spelman and transferred to Clark Atlanta. I hated to leave Spelman, but I didn't want to chance running into Julian. I hated that I had to change my whole life around, but I was willing to do anything, including changing Kadence's daycare, to keep us safe.

Julian was much more demented than Black had ever been,

and I hated to admit that I feared him because I knew what he was capable of.

Mommy talked me into getting an order of protection against Julian, he wasn't allowed to get within 1000 feet of me or he would be arrested. Everybody wanted me to press charges against Julian, but I didn't want to go through that headache. Rico bought me a pink pearl handled .22, and took me to the gun range and taught me how to shoot.

I didn't like the idea of having a gun in the house because of Kadence, so I kept it in the glove compartment in my car. I also had a stun gun that looked like a cell phone that I kept in my purse.

"SJ, what you want for dinner tonight?" I asked as I grabbed my black MCM purse.

"Whatever you cook sis," he replied, never looking up from the TV, and I shook my head.

I grabbed Kadence and headed out the door, after strapping her in we were off to the grocery store. I upgraded my car, so now I was pushing a white 2007 Acura Legend TL with deep tinted windows and black 20-inch rims. I was riding down Whitlock Avenue listening to Lil Kim's Notorious K.I.M album, when a particular song called "Hold On" ft. Mary J. Blige caught my attention. I've heard this song numerous times, but that was the first time I actually listened to the words.

"Don't you give up, be strong, hold on hold on, things are gonna get better... Tough times they last so long, hold on hold

on, if you believe they will get better..."

The words to that song spoke directly to my heart, I played it over and over again until I pulled up at the Kroger grocery store. I grabbed Kadence and as I was headed into the store I heard my name being called. Turning around, I saw Adriana coming my way, with Johnathan on her heels.

"Kaylen, I'm so glad you're ok, mami," she said, embracing me tightly.

It actually felt good to see her.

"Hey Kay," Johnathan said as he embraced me warmly.

"Hey guys, this is my daughter, Kadence," I said, smiling while picking her up.

"She's gorgeous, Kay," Adriana said making silly faces at Kadence, causing her to giggle and reach for her.

Johnathan rubbed her chubby cheeks, and to my surprise she reached for him, something she'd never done with Julian. We made small talk as Johnathan played with Kadence, I gave them my new number, and we promised to get together soon.

"Johnathan, I would appreciate if you didn't tell your brother about you seeing me," I told him.

"You don't have to worry about that, Kay, we got into a nasty fight when he called and told me what he did. Mom made every excuse in the book for him, claiming you had to provoke him because he would never do anything like that. I swear my family is so messed up it ain't even funny, I've been keeping my distance, cause I still want to take Julian's head off. You should've sent his ass to jail," Johnathan said angrily, and Kadence popped him in the mouth for his use of bad language causing us to laugh.

"My mom said the same thing, but honestly, I didn't want to go through that headache," I shrugged.

"I hope you at least got a restraining order," Adriana said with a raised eyebrow.

"Yes, I did," I nodded my head.

"Well, we won't hold you up anymore, I'll give you a call tomorrow, mami," Adriana said before hugging me.

"Bye pretty girl," She said, kissing Kadence's chubby cheeks as Johnathan did the same, and they left as we entered the store.

For dinner, I decided to try a recipe for crab stuffed chicken breast with mashed potatoes and asparagus, and for dessert I decided on my famous red velvet cake.

"Damn sis, I'm gonna hate to see you leave," SJ said, as he rubbed his stuffed belly.

"You need your space, and besides you're welcome to come by and eat anytime," I said, sitting a slice of cake in front of him.

After cleaning the kitchen and getting Kadence ready for bed, I decided to have a glass of wine and sit on the patio. SJ joined me after I had been sitting out for a while.

"You know you can tell me anything right?" he asked, sitting down next to me.

"Of course I do," I said giving him a smile as I grabbed his hand.

"Can I ask you something," he said.

"You just did," I replied sarcastically.

"Jerk," He laughed.

"You know you can ask me anything," I told him.

"Why won't you press charges?" He asked, and I sighed.

"Honestly, I'm just over it all, you know? I don't wanna go through the process of a trial and having to testify and all that, I just want him to stay as far away from me as he can. If I don't see him ever again, it'd still be too soon," I told him.

"I respect that, Kay. I don't like it, but I respect it, and if he knows what's good for him, he'll stay away from you," SJ replied.

"Anyway, enough about that, what's been going on with you?" I asked changing the subject.

"Nothing much, school and work, that's about it," he shrugged.

"Dating?" I asked.

"I mean, I have friends," he said, nonchalantly.

"So in other words, you're just screwing," I said with a raised eyebrow.

"You could say that," he chuckled as I shook my head.

"So, when you gonna give Rico a chance?" he asked, catching me off guard, and I almost choked on my wine.

"Where did that come from?" I asked.

"Come on Kay, everybody can see that you two love each other. He's been there from the beginning, and he loves Kadence as if she is his biologically. You two do everything a couple does. When he's in town, you two even sleep in the same bed. Honestly, we all thought that you and Rico would've hooked up a long time ago," he said.

"Well, I'm not trying to date anyone right now, except myself and Tootie. I gotta get back to loving me before I can ever even think about another relationship. Besides, Rico has a girlfriend anyway," I replied sipping on my wine.

"You late sis, that's a done deal," SJ said, with a smirk on his face.

"When did that happen?" I asked coolly, but I was jumping for joy on the inside.

"A few months ago," he said as his phone chimed.

"That's my cue, I'll be back later, sis," he said, kissing my cheek.

"Yea Yea Yea, make sure you wear a condom, Mommy would kick your ass if you brought her another grandbaby right now!" I said, jokingly.

"Bye Kaylen," he replied, laughing.

Gosh, I loved my brother. A few years ago I didn't even know that he existed, and now we were so close, you would've thought that we grew up together.

CHAPTER THIRTY TWO

Two Years Later...

Life was going great, I had finally graduated from CAU with my bachelor's degree in Psychology, and I couldn't have been happier. I had even landed an intern position with a local psychiatrist. Kadence was three going on thirty and smart as a whip, with the brightest personality. I hadn't seen or heard from Julian, and for that I was thankful.

I still kept in touch with Adriana and Johnathan. In fact, they made me the God mother of their daughter, Nyala. I learned from them that Julian was engaged to Samantha, and she learned the hard way that all that glitters ain't gold, but now she was in too deep.

Rico had officially moved to Georgia, along with Twon, who got out of prison early for good behavior. Everything was going great for us. Sherika and Rae were now married. They had a beautiful ceremony in Hawaii.

Black and I were actually building a friendship, which was a surprise to me, but a welcomed one. It actually felt good to have a civilized conversation with Black. When he called, I allowed him to talk to Kadence and even took her to visit him sometimes.

But you know what they say, when things are going too good, something bad is around the corner. On July 18th, 2010, Alonzo killed Mya and Little AJ, and then killed himself. I was heartbroken and distraught over it. I had talked to Mya a day prior and tried to talk her into coming to Georgia to get away from him. Not knowing, that would be the last time I heard her voice. I should've tried harder; I blamed myself a little for her death and also the death of her son.

We drove down the day before the funeral and since Mya didn't have any insurance, Rico and I paid for everything. We stayed at Daddy's house, since Mommy decided to keep it. We had to drive three separate cars to accommodate everyone comfortably. After a long ride, we finally pulled up to the house at 6:00 that evening.

"Kaylen and Rico, y'all share Kaylen's old room. Carol, you can sleep with me and I'll take Kadence too since I have that big ol bed. Sherika and Rae, y'all take the first guest room, and Twon, you can sleep in the other guest room," Mommy ordered giving out sleeping arrangements.

"Nah, Miss Karen, I can go get a room," Twon tried to protest.

"Well, that would be just crazy. You staying here, boy, we got plenty of room," Mommy told him shutting him down.

"Yes ma'am," he said, smiling at her.

"Ummmm, you forgot about me, mama," SJ whined throwing his hands up.

"Oh hush boy, ain't nobody forgot about you, you can take the other guest room with Twon, since it has those twin beds," Mommy told him then mushed him in the forehead causing everybody to laugh.

While everybody got situated, Sherika, Rae and I decided to go to the grocery store to grab enough food to last us for the week that we would be here.

"Tootie, you wanna go with mommy?" I asked her, as we got ready to leave.

"I stay with Daddy," she told me as she climbed onto Rico's lap.

"Traitor!" I jokingly stuck my tongue out at them.

"Don't hate because my baby love me," Rico said, winking at me as we left.

We piled into the truck and headed for the grocery store. Twenty minutes later, we pulled up to the Harris Teeter and entered the store.

"What we getting, Kay," Rae asked, grabbing a cart.

"Just the basics and some things to cook while we're here, plus we gotta get some snacks for Tootie," I told her. "Oh yea, and some white cheddar popcorn for Rico," I added.

"What's going on with you two anyway," Sherika asked as we peruse the aisles.

"We're just friends," I said shrugging.

"Why is that though? I mean, it's obvious that you two want each other, so why not take that step?" Rae asked me.

"I mean, of course I care about Rico, and I would love to be with him. But, I just don't feel as though my past will allow him to want me on that level," I said shrugging.

Honestly, nothing would make me happier than being with Rico, but there was a reason he hadn't crossed that line with me, maybe it just wasn't in the cards for us.

"Kaylen, Rico loves you, and I know you love him. Just take a step out on faith and see what happens," Sherika replied.

"But he hasn't taken that step, so maybe he doesn't want me that way," I said, tossing two bags of popcorn in the cart along with some fruit snacks.

"If he won't take it, then maybe you should," She suggested.

An hour and $233.76 later, we loaded everything in the truck and headed back home. The ride was fairly quiet, and I was lost in my own thoughts. Should I make the first move? It's obvious that Rico is the one I want, but what if he rejects me? Lord knows my heart can't take that, so I guess we'll just see what happens.

CHAPTER THIRTY THREE

Today was the day of Mya and little AJ's funeral. My nerves were on edge, and I was having Déjà vu. Rico went to drop Tootie off at Aunt Yvette's because I didn't want her to go to the funeral.

"Knock knock," Rae said before entering the room.

"Hey Rae," I said somberly pulling my hair into a bun.

"You ok?" She asked, and I shrugged.

"I just feel as though I could've done something to prevent this from happening. Like I could've pushed her harder to come to Georgia," I told her as my eyes watered.

"Awww Kay, it's not your fault, things happen for a reason and even though we don't understand it sometimes we have to accept it," she said and embraced me tightly.

"I know, it just hurts really bad," I said, wiping my eyes.

"I'm here if you ever need to talk, ok," she said and I nodded.

"I know I may not say it a lot, but I truly appreciate

everything you guys have done for me over the years. Without y'all, I don't know where I would be," I cried, while hugging her tightly.

"Girl please, you're family and don't forget that," Rae told me cupping my face before kissing my cheek and leaving to get dressed.

I slipped on my grey Nina Ricci pants suit with a soft pink Chanel blouse and slid my feet into my five-inch soft pink Lola Cruz open toe pumps. Giving myself the once over, I grabbed my pink Chanel clutch and made my way to the living room.

"We need to be leaving here in the next twenty minutes if we wanna make it on time," Mommy said just as Rico entered the house.

Dressed in a grey Ralph Lauren suit, white dress shirt, soft pink tie and soft pink handkerchief with grey Gucci loafers, Rico looked very handsome and matched me perfectly.

"We're ready," Sherika announced as her and Rae emerged followed by SJ and Twon.

"Lord, give us strength," Mommy prayed as we exited the house.

Rico, Mommy, Aunt Carol and I decided to ride together, while Sherika, Rae, SJ and Twon rode in another car. On the way to the same church we had my daddy's funeral, I felt myself get extremely hot, and my breath started to quicken.

"You ok mama?" Rico asked me, with concern as I started to hyperventilate.

"Pull over, Rico, she's having an anxiety attack," Mommy said, and Rico pulled into a gas station.

"Look at me, Kaylen," Mommy grabbed me and turned my face gently toward her.

"Breathe baby, just breathe, everything is gonna be ok," Mommy said, soothingly rubbing my face.

"Go get her some water, Rico," Aunt Carol said and Rico rushed into the store.

"What's going on?" Rae asked as they approach the car.

"Kaylen is having an anxiety attack," Mommy told her.

"Calm yourself down, Kay," Rae said softly, and grabbed me into a hug as Rico rushed back with the water.

I drank the water slowly, and I started to feel better.

"I'm sorry guys, it's just too much for me," I cried, breaking down again.

"You gotta be strong, mama," Rico said and pulled me into his strong embrace.

After a few more minutes, I felt a lot better, and we piled back into the car, headed to the funeral. Pulling up to the church, I took a deep breath before getting out. Rico walked around to my side and grabbed my hand.

"I'm with you every step of the way, ok," he said, and I nodded as we headed into the church.

Entering the jam-packed church, I saw Mya's soft pink casket at the front along with AJ's small grey casket, and my knees buckled slightly. Tears filled my eyes as I approached the caskets and looked at the two of them. I grabbed onto Rico tighter, as I sobbed uncontrollably and he walked me to our reserved seats.

We stood as the family entered a few minutes later, and Mya's mother, Mary Ann, broke my heart as her sobs and screams filled the sanctuary, just as a girl named Kelly started to sing, "I Know Who Holds Tomorrow."

"I don't know about tomorrow, I just live from day to day.... And I don't borrow from, it's sunshine, for its skies may turn to grey... And I don't worry, about my future, for I know what Jesus said... And today he walks beside me, for he knows what lies ahead... Many things about tomorrow, I don't seem, to under understand... But I know, I know, I know who holds tomorrow, and I, I know who holds, who holds, my hand..."

"Lord whyyyyyy my babyyyyyy," Mary Ann screamed, causing the tears to rapidly flow from my eyes.

After a few minutes, everyone from the family had entered the church and we were all seated, but the tears still rapidly flowed from my eyes as Rico pulled me close.

"Lord please give this mother and the rest of the Clark family strength to get through this tragedy. For we know that you don't make mistakes, Lord, sometimes these things happen and we don't understand them. Sister Mya and Little AJ are safe in your arms now, Lord, for their work on earth was done. Hold this family in your comforting arms, Father God, in the midnight hour when no one is around. Let the church say," Reverend

James prayed.

"Amen" everybody responded.

"Young people wake up, tomorrow is not promised. Don't let the lives of Sister Mya and her son be in vain. I see so many young women go through domestic abuse and then we end up in a setting just like this. Know your worth. It is never ok for someone to put their hands on you. That's not love. Go talk to somebody, anybody! If you're in an abusive relationship, get out now!" he preached.

The church was filled with a series of Amen's as he continued to speak. He preached a powerful sermon that touched everybody in the sanctuary.

"We will now have remarks from Miss Kaylen Gibson at this time," he said once he finished, and I made my way to the podium.

Clearing my throat, I began, "Good Afternoon."

"Good Afternoon," they replied.

"I met Mya a few years ago when I was attending NCCU, we ran into each other, literally," I said and chuckled lightly. "At the time, I was also in an abusive relationship. We were together during some very trying times. She even made me AJ's godmother, and I loved him as much as I love my daughter. He was a really special little boy, so energetic and smart. Mya became one of my best friends, and I begged her numerous times to leave and move with me, but she never would. I never thought that I would be here burying my friend at the age of twenty-two," I said as my voice started to crack.

I took a moment to gather myself.

"Take your time baby," somebody yelled out, and I wiped my tears before I continued.

"I have so many emotions running through me right now, anger, hate, confusion and most of all hurt. I was fortunate enough to escape my situation. I can only wish that I was able to help Mya escape hers. I know that God doesn't make mistakes and that things happen for a reason, but this is something I don't quite understand. Miss Mary Ann, I'm so sorry for your loss. Mya was such a beautiful person that was caught up in an unfortunate situation. I just wish that I could've prevented this," I said, as I broke down completely.

Miss Mary Ann got up pulled me into her embrace.

"It's not your fault baby," she said, tearfully and hugged me tightly as we cried together.

I had a poem to read that I wrote for Mya, but I couldn't even do it because my emotions wouldn't allow it. Rico approached us and helped Miss Mary Ann to her seat, then pulled me back to my seat where I lost control. The rest of the service went by in a blur; Mya and AJ were buried side by side. I decided not to go to the repast, so Rico took me home while everyone else went back to the church.

I removed my clothes and threw on one of Rico's t-shirts then climbed into bed. Moments later Rico climbed in behind me, kissed the back of my neck and pulled me close as I cried myself to sleep.

CHAPTER THIRTY FOUR

The next few days after the funeral went by pretty quickly, and I started to feel better. I decided to go through some of my things. I opened one of my bags and a paper fell out. Picking it up, I didn't recognize it, opening it up I saw that it's a poem entitled, "I Got Flowers Today" by Paulette Kelly. I instantly remembered the day Doctor Lynn gave it to me. I sat Indian style on the floor and began to read it.

I got flowers today.
It wasn't my birthday or any other special day
We had our first argument last night
And he said a lot of cruel things that really hurt me
I know he is sorry and didn't mean the things he said, because
he sent me flowers today...

I got flowers today.

It wasn't our anniversary or any other special day.

Last night, he threw me into a wall and started to choke me, it seemed like a nightmare, I couldn't believe it was real.

I woke up this morning sore and bruised all over

But I know he must be sorry, because he sent me flowers today...

I got flowers today

It wasn't mother's day or any other special day.

Last night he beat me up again.

And it was much worse than all the other times.

If I leave him what will I do?

How will I take care of my kids?

What about money?

I'm afraid of him and scared to leave

But I know he must be sorry, because he sent me flowers today...

I got flowers today,

Today was a very special day.

Last night he finally killed me, he beat me to death.

If only I had gathered enough courage and strength to leave him,

I wouldn't have gotten flowers today...

After finishing the poem, I had tears falling down my face.

That poem spoke volumes to me, and every other woman that went through domestic violence. I wiped my tears and made a mental note to thank Doctor Lynn for the poem. I finished going through my things and headed out of the room. I found Rico lounging on the couch watching ESPN.

"Hey big head, where's everybody?" I asked as I plopped down next to him.

"Rae and Sherika went to the mall, Ma and Aunt Carol took Tootie to get ice cream, and ain't no telling where Twon and SJ at," he replied.

We sat in silence watching the TV. Rico stole glances at me and then just watched me.

"What?" I asked with a raised eyebrow.

"You're beautiful, you know that," he said looking into my eyes as I shifted nervously.

He rubbed my cheek, while moving a stray hair behind my ear, a few seconds later I felt his soft lips on mine. I moaned slightly while opening my mouth to allow his tongue to dance with mine. Rico pulled me under him and climbed on top of me, never breaking our kiss. I ran my hands under his shirt, dragging my nails softly on his back, as he sucked gently on my bottom lip. Breaking our kiss, Rico looked down at me with so much love in his eyes, that it scared me.

"You sure you wanna do this, mama?" He asked as he lightly nibbled on my chin.

"Yes," I replied in a shaky voice.

Standing up Rico grabbed my hand, pulled me off the couch and lead me to the bedroom. After closing the door and locking it, he undressed me slowly.

Laying me gently on the bed, he steppd back and admired my body. Even after Kadence, I maintained my figure, only getting a little thicker. His piercing gaze made me slightly tremble. After he removed his jeans, he turned on the radio and Faith Evans "Tears of Joy" filled the room.

"When I think about it baby, all I can do is shake my head

Cause there ain't no explanation under the sun, oh you must be heaven sent

Wit your crazy crazy crazy crazy love, boy you got me so messed up, so messed up

Now all I know is your love, I tear up when I think about your boy, you got me so emotional but when I cry now there all tears of joy

You gotta gotta gotta understand baby, I been through so many things

My heart has seen the ups, the downs, the highs and the lows and every pain life brings

But now I got your crazy crazy crazy love and all I wanna do now is sing

Oooh, oooh, oooh, I just wanna sing for you baby

Now all I know is your love, I tear up when I think about your boy, you got me so emotional but when I cry now there all tears of joy"

Climbing on top of me, Rico began to plant kisses all over my face. Starting at my forehead, then eyelids, nose, both cheeks and finally his lips met mine. He kissed me with so much passion, he literally took my breath away.

Making his way down, he let his tongue dance on my neck, causing me to moan. He then sucked gently on my collarbone and chest, before taking my right breast into his mouth. He sucked gently on my nipple, causing my center to cream.

"Mmmmmmm," a moan escaped my lips as he clamped his teeth down gently down on my nipple, then flicked his tongue back and forth.

He then moved to my left breast and did the same, before making his way further down. Placing soft kisses on my stomach, he continued to trail my body with his lips and tongue. Trailing his way down to my feet, he lightly sucked on my toes, taking me to ecstasy. Making his way back up, he kissed my calves, legs and gently bit my thighs, before diving head first into my overflowing ocean.

"Ahhhhhh," I moaned as my back slightly arched.

Rico drove me crazy as he held my pearl in place with his teeth, then tortured me with his tongue. He slid a finger deep into my cave, he continued to assault my pink pearl with his tongue while he moved his finger in and out.

"Wait baby wait," I moaned as I attempted to push his head back.

He locked my thighs in place, and went in for the kill.

Inserting another finger as his tongue tap danced on my pearl. I could no longer contain the mind numbing orgasm, as the floodgates opened, and Rico lapped up my potion and licked me clean.

Making his way back up my body, he kissed me passionately, and I tasted my honey on his tongue. Sliding his boxers down, my mouth watered at the sight of his thick ten inches. Doing something I had never done, I slowly took him into my mouth.

Being careful not to scrape him with my teeth, I gently sucked on the tip and then took it as far into my mouth as I could. Rico tossed his head back in ecstasy, as I moved my mouth up and down while swirling my tongue around the tip. Just as I was getting into it, he suddenly stepped back.

"Did I do something wrong?" I asked with concern.

"Nah ma, you're doing everything right," he replied huskily while lowering his body onto mine.

Placing his thick head at my awaiting entrance, he pushed forward, bringing me to an instant orgasm. My mouth opened forming the perfect "O", and my eyes rolled up in my head as he rocked inside of my slowly.

"Sssssss," Rico hissed as he bit his bottom lip.

He touched places that had never been touched, as he slid in and out of me slowly.

"Look at me, Kaylen," he said sexily as I opened my eyes looking into his, as his tool found my spot.

"Uhhhhh," I groaned as he tapped my spot over and over

again.

Pulling back slightly, he placed my legs into the crook of his strong arms and picked up his pace, hitting me with a stroke so deep I literally cried as I started cumming all over the place.

"You're mine, Kay, you hear me?" He whispered in my ear, and I didn't respond, not because I didn't want to, but because I couldn't.

Turning me over, I arched my back, as he slid in even deeper than before. He grabbed a handful of my ass, as he slowly pulled out to the tip and rammed himself back in, which caused me to cry out.

He suddenly pulled out and before I could protest, I felt his thick tongue massaging my insides, bringing me to bliss once again. My whole body trembled, as he slid back into me delivering powerful strokes to my center.

"Ooooooooohhh Rico, I love you soooooo muchhhhhhh," I cried out.

"I love you too ma," he said with a voice so full of conviction and passion it caused me to buck back against him.

"Oh fuck Kay, do that shit baby," he moaned as I throwed my ass back at him.

Pulling out, he pulled me on top of him and said, "Show me how much you love me."

I did just that as I planted my feet on both sides of him, and slowly slid down on his thick pole. Winding my hips like a belly dancer, I squeezed him tightly, causing his eyes to roll up in his head. I bounced up and down like my life depended on it, as I felt another orgasm fast approaching.

Rico sat up suddenly and held me tight, while kissing me passionately, as we rocked to the beat of our own music. My toes started to tingle as an orgasm so intense rocked my core, tears rolled down my face.

Rico planted his face in the crook of my neck, and I felt him swell inside of me, before emptying his seeds deep into my fortress, as we became one and low growl escaped his throat.

"I love you Kaylen Monaé Gibson," Rico declared as he looked into my eyes, as if he were looking directly into my soul.

"I love you too De'Rico Josiah Lassiter," I replied with tears falling down my face.

Kissing my tears and holding me tightly, Rico made love to me over and over, before we fell into a deep slumber.

CHAPTER THIRTY FIVE

I woke up a few hours later, and rolled over to see that it was a little after midnight. I looked to my right and saw a sleeping Rico lightly snoring. I smiled happily and kissed his lips softly, before I headed to the bathroom.

After using the bathroom, I washed my hands and looked into the mirror. The evidence of our lovemaking was all over my neck and chest. I slipped on some sweat pants and Rico's t-shirt, then headed downstairs quietly to get me a drink.

"Ummmm hmmmm," I heard as soon as I entered the living room where I found Sherika and Rae watching a movie.

"What?" I asked bashfully.

"You glowing, Miss Lady, I guess my brother had something to do with that," Sherika said, giving me a knowing look.

"Maybe," I smirked and headed into the kitchen.

"Ain't no maybe, hoochie, it's all over your face, and neck for that matter," Rae said giggling as I blushed.

"And we heard y'all nasty asses," Sherika informed me.

"Who's we?" I asked in a panic, not wanting my mother to have heard me.

"Every damn body!" I heard from behind me, I turned around to find Aunt Carol standing there in her robe with her hands on her wide hips.

"Oh my God!" I shrieked, covering my face in embarrassment.

"Ain't no need in covering yo face, chile. Hell I'm glad it happened," Aunt Carol replied washing her hands, before cutting us all a slice of her famous five flavored pound cake.

"Well, don't keep us in suspense, was it good?" She asked sitting at the table with us.

"Spare me any details, please," Sherika replied in disgust.

"Let's just say, he made love to me not only physically, but he made love to my mental too," I told them before digging into my cake.

"Well, hot damn. Sherika, where y'all daddy at?" Aunt Carol asked seriously, causing us all to bust out laughing.

"You are too much, Auntie," I told her, shaking my head.

"Girl, I'm serious, if the son putting it down like that, then I know damn well the daddy can make it do something strange!" She said, causing us to laugh harder.

"My daddy is in prison, Aunt Carol, he got three years left though," Sherika replied, once she stopped laughing.

"That's even better, that mean when he get out, he gon be

backed up and in need of some pum cat! Hook that up, Rika boo!" Aunt Carol said.

"I absolutely can't," I replied getting up from the table.

"I'm right behind you," Rae said, while Sherika laughed so hard she had tears falling from her eyes.

"What? Chile, an old woman need some loving too," Auntie said as I washed our dishes.

"An old woman needs Jesus!" Mommy replied, coming into the kitchen.

"Why y'all down here making all this noise like it's the middle of the day?" She asked with her hands on her hips.

"Sorry mama," Sherika replied.

"Well look who finally decided to emerge," Mommy said, as her gaze landed on me.

"What you talking bout ma?" I asked her nervously.

"We came in at 6:00 and heard yo ass calling for Jesus, it's almost 1:00 and you just reappear. That man must've put in some serious work to put you in a coma like that," She responded as they all fell into a fit of laughter.

"I'm going to bed," I told them walking out, as they continued laughing.

I entered my room and found Rico half-awake watching "Belly".

"Where you been at, bae?" He asked as I removed my sweats and climbed into bed with him, snuggling close as I laid on his chest.

"Downstairs with the ladies, apparently they heard us," I told him and laughed at the look on his face.

"Mom dukes gon fuck me up!" He said, chuckling while he stroked my hair.

"They actually seemed pretty happy about it," I shrugged.

"Oh yea?" He asked surprised.

"Yea, according to them, it's been a long time coming," I told him as I yawned.

We laid in silence for a minute, lost in our own thoughts. The more I listened to the beat of his heart, the more I realized that it matched my own. At that moment, I knew that Rico was the one I had been searching for all my life.

"I love you," I told him softly.

"I love you too," he replied before rolling on top of me, entering my love cave and making love to my soul, Rico brung me to ecstasy all night long.

We stayed in North Carolina for a few more days, before we decided to head back home. I was all smiles the entire way home, I felt complete for the first time in my life, and I knew that Rico had a lot to do with that.

CHAPTER THIRTY SIX

The relationship between Rico and I was everything to me. He did things with me and paid attention to what I liked, as well as what I didn't like. He knew that I had been hurt a lot in the past, so he made it his mission to show me just how special I was.

He even convinced me to go back to church and allow God to heal my heart. I was so glad that he did, because I felt myself getting stronger spiritually everyday. I got saved and so did Rico. I made a vow to not have sex again until I was married. Rico respected my decision, and I fell even deeper in love with him. It would be hard, but I knew we had to fight temptation.

Rico had even decided to get out of the game and go legit. He opened up a few businesses and made a lot of investments. He ended up handing everything over to Twon.

Then there was the fact that he treated Tootie like she was his flesh and blood. She was so attached to Rico, that he couldn't get too far without her right behind him.

"What you wanna eat tonight, bae?" Rico asked after Mommy came and got the baby.

Rico and I didn't live together, but I found a nice little condo not far from him, so he was always at my place, or I was always at his.

"It don't matter to me, I can cook if you want," I replied.

"Nah baby, let your man take you out. You always cooking, cleaning, working, or running behind Tootie. You need a break, mama," he said.

That's one of the reasons I loved Rico so much, he made sure we went on dates all the time and tried new things.

"Well, since my man wants to take me out, how about we go to The Oceanaire?" I suggested.

"Anything for you, mama, go get dressed. I'll go home to get dressed, and I'll make our reservation." He told me.

Leaning over, I planted a juicy kiss on his luscious lips before I sashayed up the stairs.

After showering, I searched through my closet before I decided on a burnt orange BCBG bandage dress that hugged my curves dangerously. I paired it with a pair of black BCBG wedges and my short black racer jacket. I pulled my long hair into a messy bun and then added my diamond earrings and bangle bracelets. After spraying my Haiku perfume, I grabbed my purse and headed downstairs.

"Whew wee!" Rico whistled as soon as I reached the bottom.

"You look amazing, mama," He said as he pecked me on the lips.

"You don't look to bad yourself, handsome," I replied winking.

Rocking a blue dress shirt, black slacks, blue Gucci loafers, a simple black diamond cross and black diamond earrings with a fresh line up, my man was looking good enough to grace any magazine cover.

"Let's go before we get in trouble," I told him as he bit his bottom lip as he gazed at me.

"You getting thick, Kay, a nigga loving that shit, ma," Rico said as we headed to the door.

"I thought it was just me, but I noticed it too! I guess that's all them collard greens and cornbread," I laughed as Rico smacked my ass lightly.

After locking up, we headed to Rico's sparkling white Range Rover. He opened my door and then got into the truck. We hopped onto I-75 and headed towards Atlanta. Thirty minutes later, we pulled up to the restaurant, valeted and headed inside.

"Welcome to The Oceanaire. Do you have a reservation?" The hostess asked as we approached.

"Yes, we have a reservation for Lassiter," Rico replied.

"Yes sir, Mr. Lassiter, your table is ready, if you'll follow me," she said politely, before grabbing two menus as she lead us to our table.

"Your waiter will be with you shortly. Enjoy your evening,"

she said, before walking back to the front.

We looked over the menu for a few minutes before the waiter approached.

"Hello, my name is Jamison, and I will be your server for the evening. What can I get you to drink?"

"We'll take a bottle of your finest white wine," Rico told him.

"Very well sir, can I get you any appetizers?" Jamison asked.

"I'll take the fried red chili calamari," I told him.

"Excellent choice, ma'am, and for you sir?" Jamison asked Rico.

"I'm good man, thanks," Rico replied.

"I'll be back with your wine and appetizer shortly," Jamison said before he headed away from our table.

"Have I told you I love you today?" I asked Rico.

"You just did," Rico replied sarcastically and flashed me his sexy smile.

"Jerk," I said giggling, before throwing a napkin at him.

"But you love this jerk," he said as he stuck his tongue out playfully.

"More then you'll ever know," I told him and smiled.

He leaned over, and placed a juicy kiss on my lips just as our waiter returned.

"This is a Chateaux Malini '76, one of our most exquisite wines," Jamison said, placing my appetizer on the table before he filled our glasses.

"Are you ready to order?" He asked, sitting the bottle in a

bucket of ice.

"Yes I'll have the 20oz Ribeye, medium well, with the sour cream mashed potatoes, bacon braised collard greens and cream corn," Rico replied, before handing Jamison his menu.

"And for you ma'am?" He asked me.

"I'll have the seared Hawaiian Ahi Tuna with the steamed broccoli, lobster, and smoked gouda," I replied handing him my menu.

"Very well, I'll be back with your orders shortly," Jamison responded before leaving the table.

We made small talk, while sharing the appetizer before our entrées arrived. As soon as the food arrived we said our grace and dug in. We made more small talk, while stuffing our faces. We were both too stuffed for dessert, so we decided to leave.

"Baby, I'm gonna run to the restroom before we leave," I told Rico and headed to the ladies room.

Exiting the stall, I came face to face with Samantha. She didn't even look the same. I could tell Julian was taking her through hell, and I felt sorry for her.

"Kaylen, I wanna apologize for the way I acted when I first met you." She said to me while I washed my hands.

"Now I realize that Julian isn't who I thought he was," she continued as she began to cry.

"Samantha, you have to leave him, if you don't, it's only gonna get worse," I told her.

"I wished it were that easy, but it's not. My family is all

about status, Julian and I are to be married in a few months. My family would disown me if I left him now!" She cried softly.

"Is it worth your happiness? He could kill you one day, Samantha! I know we haven't been on the best of terms, but I don't want to see anybody go through what I went through. I know what Julian is capable of, you have to get out before it's too late!" I told her as I grabbed her shoulders and shook her slightly.

"Will you help me?" She asked sincerely, while looking at me with tear filled eyes.

I didn't respond right away, because honestly I didn't know how to, but then Mya's face flashed across my mind. I wouldn't be able to live with myself if something happened to Samantha after she asked for my help.

"I'll help you Samantha, but you gotta be sure you're ready to walk away," I told her.

She didn't say anything, she just turned around and pulled her dress down. There were burns, welts and bruises all over her back.

"Two days ago Julian burned me repeatedly with hot wax, beat me with a whip, then punched me over and over again on my back. I'm more than ready to walk away, Kaylen." She spoke softly and I nodded.

"Here's my number, call me the moment you're away from him," I told her placing my card in her hand.

"Thank you so much, Kaylen," she cried.

"I've been where you are, and someone helped me. I couldn't live with myself if something happened to you, and I could've helped," I said to her and then surprised myself by giving her a hug.

"Call me," I told her seriously and then walked out the bathroom.

Once I arrived back at the table, Rico stood up and ushered me out of the restaurant, but not before we walked past Julian's table. He flashed me an evil smile, and I literally saw the devil inside of him, fear quickly filled my eyes. Then I remembered I was with Rico, and I instantly felt safe. Rico glared at Julian, like he could kill him right there in this restaurant.

"I'll be seeing you, homie," Rico threatened menacingly.

Julian's eyes widened in fear, and I smirked as we headed out of the restaurant.

CHAPTER THIRTY SEVEN

After the run in I had with Samantha, I realized that I wanted to help more women like her. I reached out to Doctor Lynn, and she put me in touch with Mrs. Kerry Williamson, the director of Harbor Inc, a domestic violence shelter in Smithfield.

We had a very long conversation about what her shelter did for abused women. I immediately told her about Samantha. She informed me that Samantha was more than welcome to come. After I got in touch with Samantha, I bought her a one way plane ticket to North Carolina, wrote her a check for $10,000 and she was on her way.

After I helped her, my passion for helping women of domestic violence grew into a burning fire inside me. I quit my job and started volunteering at different shelters around Georgia.

"Babe, I've got an idea that I wanna run by you," I told Rico one night while him and Tootie were on the floor playing.

"What's up, mama?" He replied looking up at me.

"I wanna open up a domestic violence center in Mya's memory," I told him.

"I think that's a great idea, bae, you wanna do it here in Georgia, or you wanna do it back home?" He asked.

"Why not do both," I replied.

"One at a time, ma," he said, chuckling.

"I know. I'm just so excited!" I told him.

Climbing onto the couch next to me, Rico pulled me into his arms and kissed me softly.

"What was that for?" I asked him.

"Just for being who you are, ma. You could've let life knock you down, but you didn't. I mean, you were down for a minute, but you came up swinging! I think it's amazing what you're trying to do, and I'm behind you one hundred percent." He said as he gazed into my eyes.

The love I saw in his eyes matched my own. Rico was it for me, If it wasn't him, then it wasn't anybody.

Kadence climbed in between us, pushed Rico away from me then looked at me, and we fell out laughing.

"This girl is too spoiled, she wants you all to herself," I said to him.

"My daddy," Kadence said as she wrapped her little arms around Rico's neck.

"But you live with me, little girl," I told her smiling.

"You better leave my baby alone, Kay," Rico said and she started to giggled.

"And if I don't?" I asked.

Before I could comprehend what was going on, Rico lunged at me tickling me all over. Before long, I felt Tootie's little hands trying to tickle me too.

"Rico stopppppppp!" I yelled through my laughter.

"You gon leave my baby alone?" he asked.

"Nooooooo!" I screamed, laughing harder as he continued to tickle me.

"Ok ok ok, I'll leave her alone," I told him with tears rolling down my face as he finally let me up.

"Jerk," I said as I sat up and wiped my eyes.

"Mommy cry," Kadence said and glared at Rico.

I looked at Kadence, and we both jumped on Rico, hitting him all over. It was moments like that, that I treasured. One of the reasons I loved Rico so much. There was never a dull moment in our relationship.

We ate dinner, and Rico gave Kadence a bath before reading her a bedtime story, then he tucked her in. I stood at the door and watched the two of them. One would never know that Rico wasn't her birth father. Black wasn't really happy about it, but he respected Rico for stepping up and being there for her while he couldn't.

I climbed into bed after I showered, and Rico came in not long after.

"I'm leaving ma, I'll be by in the morning," Rico said, before he kissed my forehead, nose and lips.

"Stay," I told him.

"You sure?" he asked, and I nodded.

Stripping down to his boxers, Rico climbed into bed with me and pulled me close. We spent the rest of the night talking about our future, before drifting off into a peaceful sleep.

The next morning I got to work on doing research for my new project, which I was going to name, "Mya's Safe Haven". I reached out to Sherry Michaels, the realtor that sold me my condo, and she informed me that she had a few spots open that she thought I would like. Rico and Kadence tagged along as we looked at property after property, none of which I liked.

"Kaylen, I have one last property that I think you'll love!" Sherri told me.

We drove a little ways out to Tucker, Georgia. When we pulled up to the building I was instantly in love. It looked to be an old office building. The lower level was spacious, and I already envisioned the set up and layout of how I wanted everything to look. The building had a total of five floors, and the offices were huge. I would have to knock down some walls, but it could work.

"I love this place," I told Sherri after she finished the tour.

"I knew you would, so should we keep looking, or is this the one?" She asked smiling.

"This is the one!" I told her excitedly.

"This place is dope, a little renovation and it would be perfect," Rico said.

"What's the asking price?" I asked Sherri ready to get down to business.

"The asking prices is $349,500," She replied.

"I wanna put in an offer of $300,000 cash for a quick sale," I told her.

She jotted something down and then stepped outside to call the seller as we continued to look around.

"If we knocked these walls down, we could make these offices into two separate bedrooms. Then we could have a few bathrooms added, we could put two kitchens on the second level and a playroom on each floor," I explained to Rico as we walked from area to area.

Thirty minutes later, Sherri walked back in smiling.

"Ok, he's willing to take the $300,000. I explained to him what you wanted to do, and he wants to offer his company for sponsorship. The phenomenal part about that is he owns a multimillion dollar contractor company!" She said excitedly.

Look at God! I was speechless because I didn't know where to start as far as looking for a contractor and one just literally fell into my lap!

"Deal!" I told her.

"Great! I'll have the paperwork drawn up, and I'll get back with you in a few days!" She said, and we agreed before we exited the building.

I was hit with a rush of nausea out of nowhere as we got into the car. I quickly opened the door and vomited up everything I ate that morning.

"You aight, Kay?" Rico asked with concern, while he rubbed my back.

"Yea, I think it was something I ate this morning," I replied.

Rico looked at me strangely as I closed the door and leaned back in the seat. He pulled off slowly, and we headed back home, I felt sick the entire way.

I mentally calculated the last time Rico and I made love. It was almost four months ago. Then it dawned on me that I hadn't had a period in almost two months!

I couldn't be pregnant, could I?

CHAPTER THIRTY EIGHT

I went to the doctor the next morning, and I was in fact a little over three months pregnant and due on April 16th, 2011. I was in complete shock because my stomach was flat as a board, but my hips and booty were wider than all outside. A part of me was excited, but the other part of me was nervous to tell Rico. I mean, we had only been together for a short while and here I was pregnant again. Then there was the fact that Kadence was only three.

I picked Kadence up from SJ's and headed home to wait on Rico. Once we arrived home, I fixed Kadence a snack and then cuddled with her as we watched The Lion King. Rico came in just as the movie finished.

"Look at my two favorite ladies." He said, smiling before he kissed my lips and grabbed Kaylen.

"Hey baby, how was your day?" I asked him yawning.

"It was real good, how was yours?" He asked, looking at me.

"I went to the doctor today," I told him as I fidgeted nervously.

"Ok, and what happened?"

"I'm pregnant," I mumbled softly.

"What did you just say?" He asked me as he sat up.

"I'm pregnant," I repeated louder and looked at him with tears in my eyes.

He didn't say anything for a while and then he jumped up happily.

"I knew it!" He shouted happily.

"So you're not mad?" I asked him in confusion.

"Hell nah!" He said, flopping next to me and planting kisses all over my face.

"Wait, why would you think I would be mad?" He asked, and I put my head down.

"I didn't want you to think that I was trying to trap you. I swear I didn't mean for this to happen Rico," I cried, as he looked at me like I was crazy before he pulled me into his arms.

"Kaylen, that baby was made out of love, ma. I would never think that about you because I know that you would never do anything like that. I knew what could happen by making love to you without protection. This baby is a blessing, and I love you now more than ever because you're giving me something that no one else ever has," he said, before kissing my tears and then my lips.

"I love you too," I told him before giving him a weak smile.

He pulled out his phone to start making calls, and I stopped him.

"How about we wait and tell them on Christmas?" I suggested.

"Why you wanna wait?" He asked, with a raised eyebrow.

"Because by then we'll know what we're having, and plus, it's my birthday, " I said shrugging.

It took a little convincing, but Rico reluctantly agreed. We spent the rest of the evening talking about the plans for Mya's Safe Haven. We ate dinner, and I was actually able to keep it down.

I bathed Kadence and got her ready for bed. She whined when I put her in her bed, so I brought her to bed with us. After we climbed in bed, we put on Happy Feet and watched it together as a family. Well, they watched it, I was out as soon as my head hit the pillow.

I awakened the next day to an empty bed. I checked the time and saw that it was a little after eleven. I climbed out of bed and performed my morning hygiene, then headed downstairs to find an empty house.

Entering the kitchen, I found a note from Rico on the fridge letting me know that he and Kadence went to visit Sherika. I made a bowl of cereal and ate quickly before heading to take a shower.

I was scheduled to meet Sherri at 2pm to sign the paperwork for the building and get the keys. I felt like dressing up, so I put on a navy blue pin striped pants suit with a white blouse underneath. I slid my feet into my five inch, navy blue Louboutins and then pulled my hair into a neat bun and added my diamond earrings. I grabbed my purse and headed towards Atlanta to meet Sherri. Once I got on the highway I decided to give Rico a call.

"What's up, mama?" He said answering the phone on the third ring.

"Hey babe, headed to meet Sherri, what y'all doing?" I asked.

"At the mall with Sherika," he replied.

"Hey sis," I heard her say in the background, and I chuckled.

"Tell her I said hey. I shouldn't be long at Sherri's, so how about we meet for an early dinner?" I asked him.

"That's cool, you sure you don't want me to meet you at Sherri's?" He asked.

"I think I got it from here," I told him.

"Ok, call me if you need me," he said.

"I will, love you."

"Love you too, ma," he replied, and we ended our call.

I pulled up to Sherri's office twenty minutes later and headed inside. I signed the necessary paperwork and met with the seller, who's name I learned was Joseph Mackey. After exchanging contact information, she handed me the keys, and I left.

I stopped by the gas station and entered the store, and as I was standing in line, a face I never wanted to see again entered the store.

"Well hello, Kaylen," Julian said as he approached me, and I didn't respond as I rolled my eyes.

"You know it's rude to not speak, Kaylen." He said and stepped into my personal space.

"Julian, get the hell out of my face," I said, through clenched teeth.

"And what if I don't? What you gonna do, call your little boyfriend?" He asked smirking.

"Go to hell, Julian," I replied, as I attempted to walk around him, only for him to grab my arm.

"I'm not done talking to you, Kaylen." He said and gripped my arm tighter.

"You're hurting me."

"Good, now I suggest you don't make a scene, or I'll shoot you right here in this store." He said evilly.

"Now we're gonna walk out that door, and you're gonna go with me, you got it?" He said and then pulled me toward the door.

If I got into his car with him, I could guarantee that I wouldn't make it out alive. Just before we got to the door, I elbowed him hard in the nose and made a run for it.

"You bitch!" He screamed holding his bloody nose.

I hopped into my car, locked the doors and shakily started the car. Just as he ran toward me, I pulled off.

My hands were shaking so bad, I had to pull over. I grabbed my gun from the glove compartment, and I dialed Rico with shaky hands.

"What's up, mama?"

"He tried to kill me!" I screamed hysterically.

"Calm down, Kay, now explain to me what happened," he said.

I calmed my nerves a little and slowly told Rico everything that happened.

"Where are you now?" He asked.

"I'm near Washington St in Atlanta," I told him as I cried.

"Can you make it to SJ's safely?" He asked me.

"Yea, I think so," I said, looking around.

"I'm gonna stay on the phone with you until you get there, I'm headed that way now," he said.

I hopped back on the road with Rico talking to me the whole way. About seven minutes later, I pulled up to SJ's and literally ran to the door knocking like the police. As soon as he answered, I fell into his arms and sobbed uncontrollably.

"KK, what's wrong?" He asked, hugging me tightly as I continued to cry.

I heard Rico in my ear, and that was when I realized he's still on my line. I handed my blue tooth to SJ, and he began to talk to Rico. He pulled me to the couch and sat me down with his arm still around me.

"Aight bruh, I'll see you in a minute," he said and hung up the phone. "What happened sis?" He asked me with concern.

I calmed down enough to tell him what happened. The more I

talked, the more he tensed up and his jaw clenched.

"He's a dead man!" SJ shouted as he hopped up and began pacing the floor.

A few minutes later a very pissed Rico walked in, followed by a hysterical Sherika holding Kadence. Rico rushed over to me and grabbed me in a bear hold like he never wanted to let me go.

"Aye Ric, let me holla at you for a minute, bruh," SJ said.

Rico reluctantly let me go, kissed my lips and followed SJ.

"I'm so glad you're ok, sis," Sherika cried as Kadence reached for me.

I grabbed my baby girl and hugged her tightly. We sat in silence, and I was still in shock. I mean, I can't believe that Julian pulled a stunt like that in public! A few minutes later SJ and Rico emerged with murder in their eyes.

"We'll be back, stay here and don't open the door for anybody," Rico said.

"Just leave it alone, Rico! I'm ok, it's not worth it!" I jumped up from the couch and grabbed him tightly.

"He violated, Kay, for that he gotta be dealt with," Rico said calmly then kissed my forehead and walked away with SJ in tow.

I pleaded with them not to go, but my pleas fell on deaf ears as they walked out the door. I cried hysterically, scaring Kadence in the process.

"You gotta calm down, Kaylen. Julian deserves whatever they're about to give his ass," Sherika said angrily, while calming

Kadence.

"I just don't want them to get in trouble behind me and my mess," I cried.

"There was nothing you could've done or said, that would've stopped them from walking out that door. They'll be back before you know it." She replied, and I nodded.

"I'll whip us up some food, ok?" She said, and I nodded while wiping my tears.

I kicked my shoes off, and curled up with my baby girl on the couch. It wasn't long before exhaustion came over me, and I fell asleep. Sherika woke me, and we ate in silence. I looked over at the clock and noticed it was a little after 7pm, which meant the guys had been gone for a few hours.

"You heard from Rico or SJ?" I asked, and she shook her head no.

After eating, we cleaned the kitchen, and I headed upstairs to shower. I slipped on a pair of SJ's shorts and a t-shirt then climbed into bed beside a sleeping Kadence. I was out as soon as I hit the pillow.

I woke up when I felt the bed shift, I rolled over to see Rico sliding into bed beside me, no words were needed as I laid my head on his chest and he pulled me close. I fell back to sleep effortlessly, feeling safer than I've felt in a long time.

CHAPTER THIRTY NINE

Christmas was fast approaching, and I was starting to show. I was out shopping with Sherika and Rae grabbing some last minute Christmas presents.

"How's the project coming along?" Sherika asked as we entered Nordstrom's.

"It's coming along great! The renovations are scheduled to be done in January. I'm hoping for the opening to be either the middle or the end of February," I replied as I looked for gifts for Mommy and Aunt Carol.

"That's great, Kay, let us know whatever we can do to help!" Rae said.

Four hours later, I was tired and had a serious craving for cheesecake and pickles. Rae dropped me off at home, so they could get the gifts wrapped.

I entered the house to find red and white rose petals all over the floor. I walked deeper into the house, and found Rico standing by the staircase in an all-white linen suit, with Gucci loafers holding a dozen white roses. My baby was looking super sexy, with a fresh fade and two carat diamonds in his ears.

"What's all this?" I asked.

"I just wanted to do something nice for you," he replied and handed me the flowers.

"Go ahead and take your bath, your clothes for the evening are laid on the bed." He told me, and I followed the rose petals to the bathroom.

The Jacuzzi tub was filled with warm water, vanilla oil and white rose petals. I climbed into the tub after wrapping my hair and relaxed. After thirty minutes, I washed off then hopped in the shower to rinse.

I walked into the room to find an all-white flowing Emilio Pucci dress, with thigh high splits on both sides. After slipping on my undergarments, I slid the dress on, and it fit my body like a glove even showcasing my slightly protruding baby bump.

I slid my feet into the all-white Giuseppe pumps and then unwrapped my hair. I applied a thin coat of lip gloss, added my diamond earrings and headed out of the room in search of my man. I found him standing at the bottom of the staircase waiting for me.

"You look beautiful, ma." He said, kissing my lips softly, and I blushed.

"Thank you," I replied.

He grabbed my hand and led me to the candlelit table, he

pulled the chair out for me and I sat down as he joined me. We said grace and dug in to the honey glazed pork loin, garlic mashed potatoes, steamed broccoli with cheese sauce and a sautéed vegetable melody.

After dinner we shared a strawberry cheesecake, mine with pickles of course. Rico stood up from the table and shuffled through his iPod and The Temptations, "This is My Promise" filled the room.

"May I have this dance?" Rico asked me reaching out his hand.

"Of course," I told him grabbing his hand.

We began to dance slowly as he sung in my ear.

"You're a very special part of my life, you're the one that I adore. You are my cherie amour, you're the one (you're the one) I've been looking for (that I've been praying for).

I wanna love you baby, love you for better or worse. I wanna honor you baby, honor because you come first and I will cherish you, like no other man can do. This is my promise to you!

This is my promise to you (all day long baby), this is my promise to you.

There will never be another you, you would make my heart complete and I'll supply your every needs. I wanna know, will you marry me?

I wanna care for you baby, whether in sickness or health. I promise you baby, love you and nobody else.

I'll even die for you and to thine ownself I'll be true, this is my promise to you."

Rico stopped dancing suddenly and looked deeply into my eyes. Then he slowly got down on one knee, removing a ring box from his pocket. My hand instantly covered my mouth as my eyes started to water.

"Kaylen, I love you so much, ma. Without you I'm incomplete. You came in and effortlessly snatched up my heart. You are the epitome of strength. I've watched you go through so much, and each time you bounced back stronger than before. You're the air I breathe, ma. I carry you in my spirit every day. The love I have for you goes past my body and beyond my mind. I love you from the very depths of my soul. There is no me without you, you make my life complete. I love everything about you, the way you walk, the way you talk, the way you laugh, I love you. You're the one I've been looking for. If it ain't you, it's nobody. In all my twenty-six years on this earth, I've never known a love like this. I feel as though God created you especially for me. You've given me the best gift I could've ever asked for, a family. You're my best friend, my rider, my backbone, my lady, and now, I'm asking you to be my wife. Kaylen Monaé Gibson, will you marry me?" Rico asked, after he finished pouring out his heart to me.

I was left speechless, as the tears rolled down my face at a rapid speed.

"Yes yes yes!" I shouted.

Rico stood up and kissed me so passionately, I was left

breathless for a few minutes. He then slid a 14-carat rectangular cut diamond flanked by two diamonds on each side in a white gold setting onto my finger. I was admiring my ring when I heard applauding behind me. I turned around to find my family cheering and clapping with tears in their eyes.

"Let me see that ring, girl," Aunt Carol said, and they all admire my flawless ring.

I noticed Rico pick Kadence up and slide a miniature version of my ring onto her little finger. My heart instantly smiled. He was definitely the one!

Now I know I said that I was practicing abstinence, but I had to show my man my appreciation. That night Rico and I made love like we never had before. He took me to a level of intimacy that I'd never been to.

CHAPTER FORTY

The night before Christmas everybody decided to stay at Sherika and Rae's house, so we could be open our gifts together on Christmas morning. We all sat around opening our gifts and enjoying each other. I got Rico a bunch of outfits, jewelry and shoes. He handed me two small boxes and told me not open them until later.

He then handed me a medium sized box. I opened it to find an all-black Yorkshire Terrier that I instantly fell in love with. I decided to name her Diva. Kadence got everything you could possibly get for a four year old. It was time for us to give out our surprise gifts, Rico handed everyone a small box.

"Ok, we have a surprise for you all! On the count of three, I want you to all open your boxes! 1...2...3 Open!" I told them and watched their facial expressions as they pulled out a pair of baby blue baby booties.

"We're having a baby!" Rico and I shouted in unison causing

everybody to scream.

"I knew it! I knew it was a reason I dreamed about them fishes a few months ago!" Mommy cried, as she embraced me tightly.

After we ate breakfast, Rico told everybody to get dressed, so that he could give me my gifts. Honestly, I wasn't expecting anything else; the ring was enough for me. Besides, I had everything in the world I ever wanted, him and my babies.

After getting dressed, we hopped into our cars then jumped on the highway. Forty-five minutes later, we pulled up to a gated community in Sandy Springs. Rico pulled into a circular driveway, attached to a sprawling mini mansion, with a humongous fountain in the middle.

"Who lives here, babe?" I asked Rico in confusion.

"Open the box with the white ribbon around it." He replied while smiling at me.

I opened the box and found a single key. I looked from the key, to the house, then back to Rico. It finally registered as I looked from the key, back to the house, and to Rico with a smile on his face.

"You didn't?!" I shouted.

"Yes I did!" He replied, and I screamed before jumping out of the car and running toward the house.

I put the key into the lock and opened the door. I was in awe; there were two spiraling staircases on each side, marble floors throughout, and a gigantic wall-to-wall fish tank in the foyer.

The kitchen was huge with marble counter tops, cherry oak kitchen cabinets and a huge subzero refrigerator.

There were two bedrooms downstairs, along with two full bathrooms and a half bathroom. Three bedrooms were upstairs, along with three full bathrooms. The master bedroom was bigger than my entire condo and fully equipped with his and her closets, a huge bathroom and a gorgeous bay window.

There was also a guesthouse in the back with a pool, Jacuzzi and a huge fenced in backyard. I ran full speed toward Rico and rained down kisses all over his face, while thanking him over and over again.

"I got one more surprise for you," Rico said and placed me on my feet.

"There is nothing that can top this!" I replied as he handed me the other box.

"Wanna bet?" He asked smirking.

I opened the box to find a Mercedes key fab. I looked at him through tear filled eyes and screamed as I took off toward the garage. I found a fully loaded, smoke gray Mercedes Benz G Wagon, that looked to be straight off the showroom floor.

I jumped into Rico's arms again and just stared into his eyes before planting a passionate kiss on his lips.

"That's why you knocked up now!" Mommy said jokingly.

"Thank you so much, this is the best Christmas/Birthday ever!" I told him.

"Anything for you, mama, you deserve this and so much

more. This is only the beginning, ma, I've got a lifetime to show you how much you mean to me and that's still not long enough," He replied, looking deep into my eyes.

"Well hot damn, Sherika, when you said your daddy get out again?" Aunt Carol asked as we busted out laughing.

"Auntie, I don't think you ready for my old man!" Rico replied.

"Boy, what you talking? I ain't new to this, I'm true to this! Have your daddy moving to Augusta!" She said, and we laugh harder.

We stayed for a little while longer, then headed back to have Christmas dinner. That was by far the best Christmas/Birthday that I'd ever had, and it was one I would never forget.

CHAPTER FORTY ONE

New Year's came and went. I was a little over seven months pregnant, and big as a house. The renovations for the center were finally completed, and we were set to open the doors on the February 1st. I was planning our wedding also. I told Rico I wanted to wait until I had the baby, so I wouldn't look like a whale in my wedding dress.

Rico wanted to get married as soon as possible, so we set a date for May 30th, 2011.

I pulled up and admired the handcrafted sign that had, "Mya's Safe Haven" in cursive purple letters. I entered the building and was impressed with the way everything was put together. I had one of the best mural painters, Mr. Monopoly, come in and do a two sided wall mural of Mya, AJ and Rico's mother Sonja.

It was absolutely breathtaking. It was a surprise to Rico, who had no idea. I walked around and admired the plush space that looked more like a five star hotel rather than a shelter. The rooms were broken down into suites, with a bathroom in between the rooms. There were a total of forty rooms and five floors. Each room was equipped with a full sized bed, TV, dressers and nice sized closets.

The color scheme was purple and silver, it was absolutely beautiful. There was a small kitchenette on each floor with a full sized kitchen on the lower level. There was also a playroom and recreational area on the lower level.

Doctor Lynn decided to relocate to Georgia, and became the full time on site doctor for the shelter. I was so grateful to her for that; a doctor would come in handy. There would be 24-hour security on hand, seven days a week. We also had an area where people could come in and donate clothes, electronics, toys and etc.

I even got with the local community college about the ladies taking classes, if that's what they wanted to do.

As I headed back into the main area, I saw Rico pull up and I met him at the door.

"Hey beautiful," he said, causing me to blush before kissing my forehead then my baby bump.

"Hey babe, I have a surprise for you! Close your eyes!" I told him.

Rico was reluctant at first, but finally agreed. I walked Rico into the building and stood him directly in front of the mural.

"Ok, open them!" I told him.

The look on his face was priceless, his eyes watered and tears rolled down his face.

"Where did you get this picture?" He asked softly admiring the artwork.

"Sherika gave it to me," I replied, wrapping my arms around him.

Rico began to sob uncontrollably as he fell to his knees; I slowly climbed down next to him and pulled him into a loving embrace as he cried.

"I should've helped her that night!" He said through his tears.

"Rico, you were just a kid, there wasn't much you could've done," I told him, looking into his tear filled eyes.

"I killed him," He softly said and then cried even harder.

I just let him get it out because I could tell this was a breakdown that he had been holding in for a while.

He calmed down and explained that after the police ruled his mother's death an accidental death, he was furious. He bought a handgun off the street and shot his stepfather six times. He told me how he called his father hysterical; he rushed over and told Rico that he was never to mention a word about what he'd done.

His father ended up taking the charge for him, and was sentenced to fifteen years in prison for second-degree murder.

"Your father was protecting you, he knew that prison wasn't the place for you," I told him after he finished telling the story.

"You're the only person besides my father that knows the truth about what went down that night," he replied.

"We don't ever have to talk about it ever again, let the past stay where it is," I told him before wiping his tears away and kissing him softly.

"I love you, Kay."

"I love you more, baby."

The following weekend we had the grand opening, and it went off without a hitch! That day we took in five girls and seven children. It swelled my heart to be in a position where I could help somebody else.

CHAPTER FORTY TWO

April 10th, 2011 at 4:35am, I gave birth to De'Rico Josiah Lassiter Jr. My baby boy was 9 pounds 1 ounce and 20 inches long; he was Rico's twin and only inherited my hazel eyes with a head full of jet black curly locks.

Everyone arrived at the hospital and fussed over baby RJ. Kadence was jealous and wouldn't let Rico hold the baby until he promised her that she could hold him. RJ had clothes, diapers, bottles, pacifiers and everything else to last him for a few years. Being that I didn't have a baby shower, they gave me one right there in the hospital.

We were sitting around joking and laughing when a breaking news segment caught my eye.

"This is Bob Stanfield reporting live from Lake Lanier where a body was found late last night. The body has now been identified as 24-year-old Julian Green. Julian Green had been missing for a while, before his body was discovered here last

night by a fisherman. Detectives said that they suspect foul play and are working around the clock to catch the people or person responsible for this horrific crime. If you have any information contact crime stoppers. Bob Stanfield reporting live."

The news report went off, and the room was filled with an eerie silence. I looked from SJ to Rico, and they didn't show any kind of emotion.

"Karma got everybody's address," Mommy said, and everybody nodded their head as I sat in shock.

They continued to chat as if nothing happened. I said a quick prayer for Julian and decided to leave it alone. My mother always told me, don't ask questions that you don't wanna know the answer to.

Two days later, we were released from the hospital. I reached out to Johnathan to pay my condolences, he simply told me that karma was a bitch, and Julian crossed a lot of people. I felt sorry that he was dead, but another part of me was a little relieved. I knew, I shouldn't have been, but hey it is what it is.

Mommy and Aunt Carol decided to move in with me for a little while, so they could help me with the kids while Rico was away. I was happy they were there because I was exhausted! I couldn't remember the last time I had a full night of sleep.

"Go on and get you some rest, we got the babies," Mommy told me taking RJ from my arms and shooed me upstairs.

I hurried upstairs, took a shower and was out before I could fully get into the bed. I woke up and noticed that it was dark outside. I rolled over and looked at the clock to see that it was a little after 10pm. I slept for almost eight hours straight! I used the bathroom, washed my face and brushed my teeth before exiting the bedroom.

I peeked in on Kadence and found her sound asleep. I figured RJ was with Mommy and continued downstairs. I headed toward the kitchen in search of something to eat, and found a sleeping Rico stretched out on the couch with RJ resting on his chest. I couldn't help but smile at the sight of the two of them. I kissed them both lightly and entered the kitchen.

I found some left-over meatloaf, mashed potatoes, corn and rolls in the fridge. I fixed me a small plate, warmed it up and dug in.

"So you just gon grub and not fix your husband any?" Rico asked from the doorway still holding a sleeping RJ.

"Rico, put him down, he's gonna be spoiled! You remember how hard it was for us to break Kadence out of being an arm baby!" I told him.

"Chill out, I fed him then changed his diaper and we both ended up falling asleep, then you woke us in here making all this noise," Rico replied giving me a silly grin as I grabbed the baby from him.

I planted kisses all over his little face and inhaled his scent. I checked him to make sure he was dry then headed upstairs to put him in the bassinet in my bedroom. After grabbing the baby monitor, I headed back downstairs.

Rico was lounging on the sofa looking so sexy in a pair of sweats and a tank top. I sat down next to him and cuddled close, laying my head on his chest.

"What time did you get in?" I asked him.

"I got here around eight, I tried to wake you, but you just kept on snoring and drooling," he said laughing.

"I do not snore, and you haven't ever seen me drool, jerk!" I replied, mushing him in the head.

"Yea ok, whatever you say, ma!" He replied.

We settled on to the couch as Love Jones came on, which was my favorite movie ever. I know it word for word, especially the part when they're in the club and Larenz Tate recited that poem.

The movie was almost over when I heard a tiny cry come through the baby monitor. I got up and headed towards the stairs to go get my fussy baby.

"Aye Kay!" Rico called out to me.

"What's up, babe?" I asked turning around.

"You better watch that big ol thang." He replied eyeing my hips and booty that have spread majorly since becoming pregnant and having RJ.

"Boy, go to bed!" I told him before laughing.

After grabbing the baby and changing his diaper, I headed back downstairs with a now wide-awake RJ. I cuddled up against Rico as we both stared at the amazing creation that was us. He was a beautiful being that was created from our love.

"How the wedding plans coming along?" Rico asked

breaking the silence.

"Honestly, I haven't even had time to focus on them," I replied.

"You need to get to it. I'm ready to make you Mrs. Lassiter!" Rico announced flashing that sexy grin I loved so much.

"What's the rush? Why so urgent?" I asked.

"Let me tell you something. This here, right now, at this very moment, is all that matters to me. I love you, girl, and that's urgent like a muthafucka!" He responded quoting Larenz Tate from Love Jones, when he was trying to get Nina back, and sounding just like him, which caused me to fall out in a fit of laughter.

I swear it was never a dull moment with Rico. He always kept a smile on my face and in my heart. Yea, it's time I buckled down on the wedding arrangements. I couldn't wait to become Mrs. De'Rico Lassiter!

CHAPTER FORTY THREE

The day had finally arrived. Today Rico and I would be joined as one. I was a nervous wreck! I hadn't seen Rico in a full twenty-four hours, and I missed him terribly.

"It's your wedding day, mama! How you feeling?" Sherika asked as she entered my room.

"I'm a nervous wreck!" I replied.

"You shouldn't be. Today you're marrying the love of your life," she responded, and I nodded in agreement.

"Where is everybody?" I asked her.

"The guys are at SJ's getting their haircuts and everything. They're gonna get dressed there and meet us there. Daddy is on his way here, Rico still doesn't have any idea that he is out. The ladies are downstairs getting their faces done. Your glam squad will be up in a little while, so go ahead and take care of your shower and hygiene. I'll send them up in an hour." She told me, and I agreed before she left the room.

I reached out to Rico's father, Josiah, a few months ago. He told Sherika and I that he would be getting released two weeks before our wedding. We flew him out and he'd been staying at Sherika's the whole time. Rico had no idea, and I couldn't wait to see the look on his face.

After showering, I slipped on my undergarments and robe then headed back into my room. My phone chimed from across the room, and I grabbed it to see a text from Rico.

MY FOREVER: Today I'm marrying my best friend. I never thought we would be here, but I'm glad we are. I couldn't imagine my life without you in it. I love you with everything in me ma!

Tears clouded my vision as I read his text over and over again. Just like that, my nerves were gone, and I was ready to become Mrs. De'Rico Josiah Lassiter.

ME: I love you more than you'll ever know. I can't think of anybody else I'd rather take this journey with. See you at the altar!

I sat my phone down just as someone knocked on the door. I rushed to open it and there was my own personal glam squad.

"You ready to be glamorized, Miss Thang?" A feminine looking male asked.

"Yes I am, let's get this show on the road!" I replied, ushering them into the room.

"My name is Stephan, I will be your hairstylist, and this is my team. Giana will be beating your face to capacity, and Ling will be doing your nails and feet," he replied introducing me to his team.

They immediately got to work, and two hours later I was finished. Stephan turned me around, and I was amazed at the finished product. He added some tracks to my hair and filled it with long cascading curls. Giana had beat my face to full capacity, and Ling gave me a classy french tip with diamond stencils on the ring finger.

"Thank you so much!" I hopped up hugging them.

"No problem, Miss Thang. You just enjoy your day!" Stephan replied as they began to pack up their tools.

"If you guys aren't busy, I would love to have you at the wedding," I told them.

"Free food and alcohol? We're there, Miss Thang!" Stephan replied and snapped his fingers.

"Great! The wedding is at 6pm at the Ventanas on Baker St, and the reception will be held at the Hilton Atlanta," I told them.

They gathered their equipment and exited the room. I looked at the time and saw that it was a little after 4pm. There was a knock at the door as I lotioned up my body.

"Come in."

"Look at my baby! You look beautiful, Kaylen," Mommy said as she entered the room.

"Thanks ma, so do you," I replied.

She was wearing a soft coral form fitting, long flowing strapless dress with silver beading criss crossing along the front by Vera Wang.

"The car will be here at 5pm to take us to the venue. I wanted give you this." She said sitting next to me and handing me a beautiful diamond ring.

"This is the ring that your father gave to me when he first proposed to me, and I wanted you to have it. I know today is bittersweet because your daddy is not here to walk you down the aisle. I know that he's watching over you right now, and he is proud of the woman you have become." She told me as I admired the ring.

"Thank you, Mommy, I love you!" I told her and hugged her tightly.

"I love you too, baby! You need some help getting ready?" She asked me, and I nodded as I placed the ring on my right ring finger.

I grabbed my dress bag and laid it on the bed, before carefully removing the dress. I had a custom made strapless mermaid styled dress. It had hand embroidered beading and Swarovski crystals wrapped around the waist. What I loved about the dress was that it wasn't your traditional white, the bottom half was dipped in a coral color, it started very light and got darker toward the bottom of my three foot train.

Mommy helped me slip into my dress that fit my curves like a glove. She then helped me place the diamond tiara onto my head. I slid my feet into my white Giuseppe open toed pumps and stood in front of the full-length mirror.

Tears filled my eyes as I took in my appearance. This was really happening!

CHAPTER FORTY THREE

New Beginnings

"I'm honored that you would allow me to walk you down the aisle and give you away. I'm so glad that we found each other, I can't imagine not having you in my life, no matter how much you get on my nerves!" SJ told me as we prepared to walk down the aisle.

He looked rather handsome in his all white tuxedo and coral colored tie.

"I love you too, big head!" I replied kissing him on his cheek as I placed my veil onto my head.

"Five minutes, Kaylen!" My wedding director, Sasha, told me.

I grabbed my bouquet and latched on to SJ's arm.

"You ready?" He asked me.

"Let's do it!" I replied smiling up at him.

We walked to the door where we met up with Sasha and

waited on our cue. Tamela Mann's "Heaven" started to play and Sasha gave us the go ahead.

"Every time I look at you I, feel something brand new it's real I can feel it all over me.

Chemistry's off the chain you, send fire through me when you call my name, has me looking forward to the last time we'll go out and hang.

Something magical happens every time I'm lying in your arms, the feeling that it gives me can, weather any storm.

Lying next to you relaxes me, makes me feel so complete yeah, no other place I'd rather be than here, here with you.

Your skin touching mine and to me you're one of a kind, I believed my search was over when you came by"

Tears filled my eyes the closer I got to Rico. I locked eyes with him and noticed that his eyes were filled with tears too. No one and nothing else mattered at this moment.

"Friends, we have joined here today to share with Kaylen and De'Rico in an important moment in their lives. In their time together, they have seen their love and understanding of each other grow and blossom, and now they have decided to live out the rest of their lives as one," Pastor Sutton said as we stood before him.

"Who gives this woman to be wed?" He asked.

"We do," Mommy and SJ replied.

SJ kissed my cheek and placed my hand into Rico's before taking his place behind Rico.

"I require and charge you both, as you stand in the presence of God, before whom the secrets of all hearts are disclosed. Having duly considered the holy covenant you are about to make, you do now declare before this company your pledge of faith, each to the other. Be well assured that if these solemn vows are kept inviolate, as God's Word demands, and if steadfastly you endeavor to do the will of your heavenly Father and earthly Mother. God will bless your marriage, will grant you fulfillment in it, and will establish your home in peace," Pastor Sutton began.

"Rico, will you have this woman as your wedded wife, to live together after God's ordinance in the holy estate of Matrimony? Will you love her, comfort her, honor, and keep her in sickness and in health; and, forsaking all others, keeping yourself only unto her, so long as you both shall live?" He asked Rico.

"I will," Rico replied looking into my eyes.

"Kaylen, will you have this man as your wedded husband, to live together after God's ordinance in the holy estate of Matrimony? Will you love him, comfort him, honour, and keep him in sickness and in health; and, forsaking all others, keeping yourself only unto him, so long as you both shall live?" He asked me.

"I will," I replied.

"Kaylen and De'Rico have chosen to say their own vows. Go ahead Rico," Pastor Sutton said.

Looking into my eyes, Rico took a deep breath before

261

beginning.

"Kaylen, I love you so much, ma. The day you came into my life, you made my world complete. I've watched you get knocked down time after time, and each time, you got back up stronger than ever. Your strength is my motivation, I promise to be faithful and supportive and to always make our family's love and happiness my priority. I will be yours in plenty and in want, in sickness and in health, in failure and in triumph. I will dream with you, celebrate with you and walk beside you through whatever our lives may bring. You are my person—my love and my life, today and always." Rico said to me with so much love in his voice, tears rolled down my face, and he wiped them away.

"Rico, I love you more than words can express. You have been my best friend, mentor, playmate, confidant and my greatest challenge. But most importantly, you are the love of my life, and you make me happier than I could ever imagine, and more loved than I ever thought possible. You have made me a better person, as our love for one another is reflected in the way I live my life. So I am truly blessed to be a part of your life, which as of today becomes our life together." I told him as the tears he so desperately tried to hold on to rolled down his face.

"Can we have the rings please?" Pastor Sutton asked.

Sherika took my bouquet and handed me the ring as Twon gave Rico his.

"Repeat after me, Rico. I, De'Rico, give you, Kaylen, this

ring as an eternal symbol of my love and commitment to you."
He said and Rico repeated before sliding the ring onto my finger.

"Repeat after me, Kaylen, I, Kaylen, give you, De'Rico, this
ring as an eternal symbol of my love and commitment to you."
He said and I repeated before sliding the ring onto his finger.

"By the power vested in me by the State of Georgia, I now
pronounce you husband and wife. De'Rico, you may now kiss
your bride," Pastor Sutton said.

Rico grabbed me by my waist and laid a kiss so passionate on
me, I swore I saw all the colors in the rainbow.

"I now present to you Mr. and Mrs. De'Rico Josiah Lassiter
Jr!" He said, and everybody stood to their feet applauding.

SJ laid a broom in front of us, and we jumped, it was official,
I was married!

On the way to the reception, Rico and I started our
honeymoon a little early, if you know what I mean! We pulled
up to the reception hall, and we were announced as our wedding
party entered. We partied the night away, and it was time for our
toast.

The sound of a clinking champagne flute caught our
attention, and the look on Rico's face was priceless as his father
stood in front of our table. As they embraced for the first time in
almost fifteen years, there wasn't a dry eye in the building.

After that, we really partied. The night took a turn for the
worse for me when the DJ played Luther Vandross "Dance With
My Father". Before a tear could even fall, Josiah grabbed my

hand and pulled me to the floor.

"I know that your father isn't here anymore, but if you'll allow me, I'd like to be a father for you," Josiah told me as we danced.

"I'd like that," I told him with tears in my eyes as we continued to dance.

After the dance, it was time to cut the cake, which Rico smashed all in my face! The night was magical and more than I could've ever dreamed of. We were set to honeymoon in the Dominican Republic, and I couldn't wait.

"So Mrs. Lassiter, you ready to make some more babies?" Rico asked me as we danced.

"I don't think so Mr. Lassiter, we got two babies already. I think that's enough for now," I replied smiling up at him.

If someone had told me that Rico was my soul mate years ago, I would've laughed! But now I realized that what we want isn't always what we need. It took me going through hell to get to heaven. When you're young, you have your whole life planned out, and it doesn't dawn on you that it's not gonna end up like that.

Mya's Safe Haven was doing very well, and we were in the process of opening one in North Carolina. My kids were healthy, and I had a man that loved me more than he loved himself. My life was complete, and I finally found my happily ever after. I had been through more than any young woman should've ever been through, but I refused to let it defeat me.

You may read my story and feel sorry for me, well don't, the things I went through made me who I am. If you're going through an abusive relationship get out while you can! Some women weren't as fortunate as I was; some lose their lives at the hands of their lovers.

Don't be ashamed to tell somebody what you're going through, things that are covered up don't get healed. These types of situations happen every single day. Get out now before it's too late!

I fought back and reclaimed my life, I was a SURVIVOR!

The End!

80432975R00152

Made in the USA
Lexington, KY
02 February 2018